Ann Aurelia
and Dorothy

DEBI GOODMAN

Ann Aurelia
and Dorothy

BY NATALIE SAVAGE CARLSON

Pictures by Dale Payson

A YEARLING BOOK

For Timothy, John, Mary Evelyn,
Todd, Pam, and Jeannine Mortimer

Contents

I	*Zing!*	1
II	The Special Drink	11
III	The Supermarket	26
IV	The Safety Patrol	40
V	The P.T.A. Meeting	57
VI	The Nature Walk	65
VII	Hallowe'en	81
VIII	The Surprise Party	95
IX	The Unexpected Visitor	108
X	The Apartment	122

Ann Aurelia

and Dorothy

I

Zing!

Zing! That's the way it happened. Just like that.

Ann Aurelia Wilson was on the playground all by herself. Of course there were other children there, and a
woman was reading a book on the green bench. The boys
were playing baseball at one end. That is, they were playing in between the times they were arguing about who
was up to bat next or whether somebody was safe or out.
Some small children were sitting in the sandbox, building
roads or throwing sand.

But Ann Aurelia was all alone, and that's the way it
had been most of the summer. She pumped higher and
higher in the swing, with her head back so the wind could
blow across her face and ruffle her short-cropped hair.
Her legs, covered by worn denim slacks, were thrust
straight out. Her sweat shirt hung shapelessly.

Ann Aurelia didn't see the little Negro girl taking a shortcut past the swing. She was a spindly little girl with hair in two exact braids and horn-rimmed glasses that had slipped halfway down her nose.

Just as the Negro girl crossed in front of the swing—*zing*—the chain broke and Ann Aurelia thumped into her. Both girls sprawled in the scrabbled dirt.

"Oops!" exclaimed Ann Aurelia. "Sorry! Did I hurt you?"

The Negro girl picked up herself and her glasses. "Nope. Didn't break my glasses either. I busted them twice already."

"And I sure busted the swing," said Ann Aurelia.

Both girls dusted themselves off, and Ann Aurelia straightened the stiffly-starched bow in back of the other girl's blue gingham dress.

"What's your name?" she asked.

"Dorothy."

"Dottie?"

"Just plain Dorothy. That's what everybody calls me. What's yours?"

"Ann Aurelia."

"Both?"

"Yep."

"Not Ann or Aurelia?"

Ann Aurelia shook her head. "I was named after two grandmas who didn't like each other. So they couldn't call me just Ann or just Aurelia because the other would get mad."

"I knew you were a girl all the time. You live near here?"

"Down that street. I live with Mrs. Hicken now. First I lived with Mrs. Jolly. She's the one got my hair cut short so it wouldn't be so much trouble to wash and comb. I like it this way. Sometimes I can play with boys a long time before they find out I'm a girl. They'd probably never find out if it wasn't that I can't throw a ball over-handed."

"Why did you leave Mrs. Jolly? She sounds like fun—her name, I mean."

"Her married daughter moved in with her children. So the agency put me with Mrs. Swann. Her husband was nice. He used to give me money for candy, but Mrs. Swann would make me hand it over to her because he never gave her half enough to buy the groceries."

"Where's your real honest mother?"

Ann Aurelia's face hardened and tightened. "Out west. But she's not caring where I am, so I'm not caring where she is."

Dorothy realized that she had touched a sore subject.

3

"You like this Mrs. Hicken? Is she nice to you?"

"She's the best. She lets me eat sandwiches in bed. She even lets me make them myself—out of whatever's in the refrig. Last night I had a baloney on rye with some hot peppers and peanut butter and strawberry jam that was left over." She paused dramatically. "And then I gooped whipped cream all over it and ate it with a spoon."

Dorothy's eyes behind her thick glasses grew even bigger with admiration. "I sure can see that sandwich even without these glasses."

"Let me have a look through them," said Ann Aurelia, stretching out her hand. Dorothy obligingly pulled off her glasses and handed them over.

Ann Aurelia put them on with a flourish. "*Zowie!* Everything looks big and blurred."

"I started out with them in first grade. Before that I thought everybody had nothing in back of them."

Ann Aurelia took a few hesitant steps over the crab grass, her hands held out as if she were walking a tightrope. Then she primly folded her arms and lifted her freckled nose into the air. "I'm Miss Watson from the agency now." She spoke in a voice as deep as she could drop it. " 'Mrs. Hicken, you may find Ann Aurelia a spirited child but she *can* be controlled.' I heard her say that when I was listening from the kitchen."

Dorothy fizzed with giggles. "You sure are a case. I

4

think you're just the most fun. But you better give me back my glasses. Mama said she'd blister me if I broke them again."

"Mothers!" scoffed Ann Aurelia, returning the glasses. "Who needs them?"

"I'm used to mine so I wouldn't want to keep changing from a Mrs. Cut-off-your-hair to a Mrs. Hicken-Chicken."

Ann Aurelia shook with an exaggerated mirth. "Dorothy, you're just the funniest yourself. When you came by, something went *zing* inside me."

"Me too."

"Bet we can have a lot of fun together."

"Sure will."

"What shall we do first?" asked Ann Aurelia.

"Maybe we can fix this old swing and pump up together."

"Okay. But the link's rusted through."

"If we could find a piece of rope or wire—"

"If there was anything like that loose around here, the boys would have gone off with it," reasoned Ann Aurelia.

"I've got a big idea," said Dorothy. "What about using my handkerchief? It won't get dirty, will it? Because my Aunt May gave it to me on my birthday."

"I'll rub off the links first with my sweat shirt. It's got to go into the wash sometime."

Ann Aurelia stretched the bottom of the shirt and

stooped to rub the links with it. Then Dorothy pulled her handkerchief into sharp points and threaded them through.

"I'll tie the knot," offered Ann Aurelia. "There was a Boy Scout lived next door to the Swanns, and he showed me how to tie a knot so it won't come loose. He wanted me to join the Scouts too, at first."

She deftly made the knot. Then she cautiously took hold of the chains and stepped up on the board seat.

"It's holding, Dorothy. I knew it would. You get on too, and see if it'll hold both of us."

"Okay, A.O."

"A.O.?"

"For Ann Aurelia. It's faster that way."

"Aurelia doesn't begin with *o*. It's *A-u-r-e-l-i-a*."

"Okay, A.A. It's a jawbreaker no matter how you spell it."

"My Grandma Wilson must have been named after somebody else too. Now let's shut up and save our breath to pump."

The children squatted and stretched themselves in turn as they pulled against the chains with their hands and pushed against the board with their feet. Higher and higher into the air they went. Dorothy's blue skirt ballooned in the wind and Ann Aurelia's slacks tightened over her knees.

6

"We've sure got her going," panted Ann Aurelia. "Bet riding in an airplane is just like this."

"Maybe we can make us go all the way over," gasped Dorothy. "I saw a man in the circus do it one time."

"We'll loop-the-loop."

Perhaps the swing would have looped-the-loop if it had been in good condition. The knot in the handkerchief still held, but there was an agonizing *ri-i-ip!* The board swung loose at one end. Dorothy flapped into the air like a young bluebird learning to fly. Ann Aurelia clung desperately to one chain like a mountain climber on a rope.

The woman on the green bench screamed and threw her book into the air. The boys stopped playing ball and came running over. Some people no one had seen before appeared as if by magic.

Dorothy lay in the sparse grass. She lay very still with one arm and one leg thrown out like a doll that is tired of being played with.

Ann Aurelia brought the swinging chain to a halt and jumped from it. She ran to Dorothy and dropped on her knees. She shook her frantically.

"Wake up, Dorothy!" she begged. "Please wake up! We don't have to play on the swing anyhow. Let's go down the slide."

Sharp fingers dug into Ann Aurelia's shoulders. They pulled her to her feet.

"Never touch anyone who's been injured," scolded the woman who had been sitting on the bench. "You might make things worse."

"They're calling the ambulance," announced a man in a straw hat. "Everybody stand back so she can get air. Stand back, sonny," he ordered Ann Aurelia.

"Who is she?" the woman asked Ann Aurelia. "What's her name?"

"Dorothy."

"Dorothy who?"

"I don't know. Just plain Dorothy."

"Where does she live?"

"Don't know that either. She never said. I didn't even think to ask her."

They heard the screeching of the siren before they saw the white ambulance. It swerved around the corner, its red dome-light flashing like a firecracker about to go off. It pulled up to the curb. Two men in white jackets jumped out. They opened the doors in back and quickly brought out a stretcher.

"Stand back, everybody," ordered one of the men. "Make way."

Ann Aurelia stepped farther back. She stood watching

the men ease Dorothy onto the stretcher. She watched them carry her to the ambulance. Then the doors closed and one of the men got in front. The ambulance shot away. Ann Aurelia could hear its long drawn-out siren fading into the distance—like a yelping dog beaten in a fight.

The people who had gathered from nowhere disappeared. The boys returned to their ball game, loudly arguing about who was up at bat when the excitement happened.

Ann Aurelia bowed her head in loneliness. Then she saw the horn-rimmed glasses lying in the grass. She picked them up. Broken glass fell out of one side. The other was neatly cracked.

Ann Aurelia sat down in the grass with her knees drawn up and her head between them. She sniffled a few times, then wiped her nose on a slack leg.

"What's the matter?" asked the woman, who had returned to the bench and was trying to find her place in the book. "Were you hurt too?"

Ann Aurelia shook her head between her knees. "They're all gone," she said, her voice muffled by the slacks. "And now Dorothy's gone too."

She pressed the broken glasses tightly against her sweat shirt.

II

The Special Drink

Mrs. Hicken was a comfortable-looking woman. You knew that she liked spaghetti and pastry just by looking at her. She was sitting in a big overstuffed chair that matched her when Ann Aurelia came in the door with a loaf of bread in her hands.

"It's come!" shouted Ann Aurelia, looking at the newspaper that Mrs. Hicken was reading. "I've been waiting for it, and now it has to come just when I've gone after the bread."

"What's come, dearie?"

"The paper," cried Ann Aurelia. She was itching to grab it from Mrs. Hicken's hands, but that wouldn't be polite. "Does it say anything about a little colored girl named Dorothy getting killed on the playground—or hurt?"

"A friend of yours? I noticed you've been in the dumps since yesterday."

"She was for a little while until the swing broke."

Mrs. Hicken was not one to give up her newspaper, especially when she was so comfortably seated for reading it.

"Old Mrs. Hentzler died, but her time had come. She's the mother of Fred Hentzler, runs the bakery. Must have been hard for her to leave all those pies and chocolate eclairs."

"But Dorothy! Doesn't it say anything about her?"

Mrs. Hicken rustled the paper. "I'll look in the accident column. Here we are!

WILLIAM COMPTON, AGED ONE, 135 SECOND STREET, WAS TAKEN TO THE HOSPITAL BY THE AMBULANCE AT 11:30 A.M. YESTERDAY AFTER HE SWALLOWED A SCREW. AT THE HOSPITAL, DOCTORS DISCOVERED HE WAS SUFFERING FROM MEASLES. HE WAS DETAINED THERE.

Now isn't that something! Had to swallow a screw for his parents to find out he had measles."

"Dorothy!" cried Ann Aurelia. "Isn't Dorothy there too?"

"This must be her."

DOROTHY GRANT, AGED TEN, OF 62 WEST STREET, WAS
TAKEN TO THE HOSPITAL AT 3:30 P.M. YESTERDAY
AFTER A FALL FROM A SWING ON THE PLAYGROUND.
SHE WAS TREATED FOR A BUMP ON THE HEAD AND RE-
LEASED.

Ann Aurelia was overcome with joy. "She's alive and she's all right. And West Street isn't far from here. Can I go to see her right now, Mrs. Hicken? I have to give her back her glasses."

"No reason you can't, dearie, but be sure to get home by four o'clock. I've got to take you to the dentist. Miss Watson is real strict about such things."

"I'll be back," cried Ann Aurelia, throwing the loaf of bread onto a chair before she raced out of the door.

She began racing down the street, but slowed to a walk when she ran out of breath.

The houses crowded closer together and drew nearer to the sidewalk as Ann Aurelia approached West Street. She quickened her steps again. It wasn't far to Number 62 now. It was a neat one-story house with a hydrangea bush filling the tiny square of yard.

Ann Aurelia hurried up the steps and knocked on the door. A slender Negro woman, with straight black hair drawn into a bun high on her head, answered.

"Does Dorothy live here?" asked Ann Aurelia breathlessly.

"Come in, little boy," invited the woman, opening the screen door. "She's sweeping her room now."

"I'm a girl."

"That's all right. You can come in anyway."

Dorothy appeared from the shadowed inner door. There was a big white bandage on her forehead. She squinted at Ann Aurelia; then went closer and stared in her face.

"It's A. A.," she cried happily. "Thought maybe you were somewhere in the hospital too. We sure had us a swinging."

"I'm okay. Mrs. Jolly used to say I had a charmed life— seeing all the things that happened to me. I brought your glasses back." She pulled them out of her pocket. "But they're busted worse than the swing."

"Thank goodness," said Dorothy's mother. "I looked all over the playground for them before dinner last night. I'll take them straight down to the optometrist. Dorothy can't half see without them. You stay and play with her. She'll have to watch Louise while I'm gone."

For the first time, Ann Aurelia noticed the little girl standing near Dorothy. She was a plump child, with her little round stomach pushing her belt up and a finger in her mouth.

"She's my little sister," explained Dorothy. "Take your

14

finger out of your mouth, Louise, and say 'howdy' to my friend."

Louise took the finger from her mouth long enough to repeat 'howdy' then put it back again.

"I won't be gone too long unless there are some ahead of me," said Mrs. Grant. "Dorothy, you make up some fruitade for—what's your name, little girl?"

"Ann Aurelia, after my grandmas."

"Ann Aurelia who?"

"Wilson. That was my father's name when he was alive."

"Well, fix some fruitade for all of you, Dorothy. Don't spill any on the kitchen floor. I just washed it this morning. And clean up after you."

She put the glasses in her handbag and went out of the door. Ann Aurelia and Dorothy stood staring at one another.

"Does it hurt under the bandage?" asked Ann Aurelia.

"Nope, but there's a bump big as a walnut. See!" She pulled off the bandage. "I don't really have to keep it on, but it makes everybody treat me nicer."

Ann Aurelia was impressed. "You've sure got a good one. It's as big as the one I got the time I fell off Mrs. Jolly's roof when I was playing with the boys. But I didn't get to ride in an ambulance like you did. Oh, I was ban-

daged and home before I knew what happened. Mr.
Jolly brought home a gallon of ice cream, and he let me
eat all I wanted."

Dorothy slipped the bandage back in place. "And
maybe Daddy will bring me some ice cream."

"I thought I'd lost you for good," said Ann Aurelia. "I
don't have any other friends. It's hard to make friends
when you move to a new place in the summer. I used to
live on the other side of town."

"I guess it must be. I've lived right here all my life."

"We'll probably go to the same school."

"Sure will. It's Jefferson."

"I'll be in fifth grade."

"Me too. We'll be in Miss Bennett's room. Everybody's
crazy about her. She's so nice and pretty. Last year I had
Miss Wyckoff. *Glap!* She's almost a hundred years old.
Even Hughie went to school to her. He always said she's
a nightmare."

"Who's Hughie?"

Dorothy pointed to the photograph on the mantel-
piece. It was of a young Negro man in Navy uniform.
"He's my brother. He's off on the west coast now. Sure
looks swell in his uniform. Even the girls who didn't use
to like him go for him now when he's home."

"You're lucky with a big brother and little sister.

There was a boy put out with Mrs. Jolly, too, but he wasn't my brother."

"I've got a big sister too. Shirley. She works in the five-and-ten and pays board to Mama and Daddy. She always gives me a quarter on payday. Let's get busy with the fruitade. Good thing I don't need glasses for the directions. I've made it so much all summer."

Ann Aurelia followed Dorothy into the small kitchen, and Louise tagged along. Ann Aurelia's sharp eyes took in the gas stove which, although very old, was clean and tidy. Not like Mrs. Hicken's with blobs of grease blackened on the burners and dark places in the grooves of the knobs. Or like Mrs. Swann's kitchen that was so clean you couldn't even make a sandwich unless you washed the butter knife before you ate the sandwich. It was more like Mum's kitchen, with the pot of something that smelled so good simmering on the back burner, and the matching dish towels with little cutouts of radishes and carrots sewed in the corners.

Dorothy set the broom in the corner and went to the refrigerator.

"You get the fruitade," she ordered Ann Aurelia. "It's on the bottom shelf there with the dry soups. Take whatever flavor you want."

While Dorothy pulled out the ice tray and pinched out

17

the cubes, Ann Aurelia looked through the colored packets. "Let's try cherry. I like cherries. One time I ate a whole big bag of them by myself. Boy, was I ever sick! I swallowed most of the pits too."

"A. A., I'm thinking we don't want plain fruitade. Let's make something special like you did with the sandwich."

"Suits me. What have you got in the refrig besides that ice?"

Dorothy swung the door open again. "What's that bottle? I can't see without my glasses."

"It's catsup."

"I never had a drink with catsup in it, did you?"

"I've had tomato juice but it wasn't in any cherry drink," admitted Ann Aurelia.

"Let's try it. Not too much though."

"Here! I'll just drop in a blob. Oops! That's more than I meant. I think we got too much."

"Then we ought to put something else in to kill the taste," suggested Dorothy. "I know that's apple butter in this jar."

"Looks like it. That ought to thicken it some. Where's a spoon?"

"In that top drawer."

Ann Aurelia spooned apple butter into the pitcher while Dorothy stirred vigorously.

"It doesn't mix right," complained Ann Aurelia.

"Maybe we could use the eggbeater on it," said Dorothy.

She fumbled for the eggbeater in the lower drawer. She whipped the drink into a froth.

"Mrs. Swann used to beat an egg into milk that way every morning for Mr. Swann," said Ann Aurelia. "He liked eggnog."

"Why don't we whip up an egg in this as long as we've got to wash the eggbeater anyhow?"

"Why not? If it was good enough for Mr. Swann, it ought to be good enough for us. He was real finicky."

Dorothy cracked the egg on the rim of the pitcher. "Oh, oh! Some of the shell went in too."

"That won't matter."

Dorothy frowned. "It looks muddy. Maybe it's because I don't have my glasses."

"It's no particular color at all."

"Mama has some food coloring in the closet. Why don't you pick out a color you like?"

Ann Aurelia examined the little bottles. "There's red and yellow and blue and—"

Louise spoke for the first time. "I like blue."

"I never did drink anything blue," confessed Ann Aurelia, "not even medicine. Let's make it blue like Louise wants."

Dorothy churned the eggbeater awhile longer. "It's

still a funny color."

"We don't care. We better put a lot of sugar in it to sweeten up all that egg and catsup."

"There's maple syrup in the cupboard. It's even better than sugar."

After the syrup was added, both girls studied the pitcher thoughtfully.

"It looks awful," said Ann Aurelia.

"We'll try it on Louise first," decided Dorothy. "You want some of this yummy, scrumptious, special drink, Louise?"

The little girl took her finger from her mouth and nodded eagerly.

Dorothy selected a glass from the cupboard and poured it full of the mixture. She handed it to her sister. She and Ann Aurelia stood staring intently at the child as she slowly downed the drink. When it was gone, Louise looked into the empty glass. Then she held it out.

"More," she ordered.

The older girls were delighted.

"We've invented a new drink." Dorothy began a jerky little dance between the sink and the refrigerator. "*A-poof! E-poof! I-poof!*" she chanted.

Ann Aurelia joined her, hopping stiffly from one foot to the other. "*O-poof! U- and I-poof! We've poofed a brand new drink nobody's ever had before."

"Nobody but Louise. Let's poof some of it into glasses for us."

She did so after refilling Louise's glass. "We'll poof us a party."

Each girl took a slow sip.

"It tastes funny," said Dorothy, "but it's sweet enough."

"Anything this sweet ought to be good."

They slowly drained their glasses.

"Want more?" asked Dorothy.

"It's pretty rich. Maybe we ought to wait awhile."

"Better we let it settle and do something else before we drink more. You want to peek into Shirley's room and see all her stuff? She's got the most clothes. Sometimes I try them on when she's gone."

Ann Aurelia followed Dorothy into a tiny pink bedroom. The skirted dressing table and a bed covered with a rose print almost filled it. Ann Aurelia was most interested in the dressing table.

"Mum had one just like this. And she had about a hundred kinds of lipsticks."

"So has Shirley, and a lot of other gook too. What did your mum look like?"

Ann Aurelia hesitated a moment, then she said, "She had eyes like violets and lips like a rosebud and—and—she walked with a regal air."

Dorothy stared. "You don't say! Shirley doesn't look

anything like that, but she's real pretty. Oh, we better get out of here! I hear Mama coming in the front door. I'll show you Shirley's clothes some other time. We can both try them on."

"*Oops!* I bet it's late. I've got to get myself home. Have to see the dentist at four."

"I'll walk a way with you."

"Will you? That'll make it go faster."

Mrs. Grant smiled at them. "Did you children have a good time? Did you have enough fruitade?"

"Yes," answered Dorothy. "We made more than enough. Maybe Louise can finish it off. She likes blue."

"Did you clean up your mess?"

Dorothy's look of surprise was mixed with shame. "We forgot."

"We'll do it right away," offered Ann Aurelia. "I'm in no hurry to get to the dentist."

Mrs. Grant sighed. "Run along, both of you. I'll do it myself. But remember what I'm always telling you, Dorothy. This is positively the last time."

"I'll wash the dinner dishes tonight," said Dorothy. "I'll even scrape them. And you better eat everything on your plate, Louise, or we'll never make you a special drink again."

The girls walked up the street arm-in-arm.

"We'll get together tomorrow, won't we?" asked Ann Aurelia. "We've got to get in a lot of playing before school starts."

"Really, truly, A. A.? You don't care if I bring Louise, too, do you? I have to mind her a lot of the time."

"Sure. Bring her. She's a great little kid. Not a bother like most of them. And she liked our drink."

"She really liked it better than me," Dorothy confessed. "One glass was enough."

"Enough for me too. Next time we'll leave out the catsup and the egg."

"And put real sugar in it instead of syrup."

Ann Aurelia hung her head and kicked a pebble along the sidewalk.

"I didn't tell you the truth, Dorothy," she confessed. "My Mum really doesn't have eyes like violets and lips like a rosebud. And she doesn't walk with a regal air because I don't even know what that means. I read it in a poem once. She really has sort of orange-colored hair, and she pastes on her eyelashes. One time I made a moustache on my face with them. I looked just like a man movie star, but did I ever get a licking!"

"That's okay about your mum, A. A.," said Dorothy. "Shirley doesn't look too great before she puts all that gook on her face either."

25

III

The Supermarket

Dorothy arrived at Mrs. Hicken's house without Louise.

"Mama took her downtown to get some new shoes," she explained, "so we don't have to be bothered with her."

"What shall we do?" asked Ann Aurelia. "Want to play cards? I have a deck of Old Maid."

Before she could go for the cards, Mrs. Hicken came in from the store with a bag in her arms.

"This is my new friend, Dorothy," said Ann Aurelia.

"Isn't she the one who was carried away in the ambulance?" asked Mrs. Hicken, still short of breath from the effort of going to the store. "She looks right chipper now."

"Here's what's left of the bump." Dorothy pointed to her forehead.

"You really got a good one," admitted Mrs. Hicken, "but it's lucky you didn't turn out to have the measles too."

Dorothy looked puzzled. "I never heard of anybody getting measles from falling out of a swing."

Ann Aurelia explained. "There was a little boy taken to the hospital too, and it turned out he had measles. That's what we read in the paper when we were looking for your name." She turned to Mrs. Hicken. "Dorothy and I will be going to school together."

"Now that's nice," said Mrs. Hicken. "You won't be lonesome the first day."

"My mother was secretary of the P.T.A. last year," boasted Dorothy to Mrs. Hicken. "Will you join it now you have A. A.?"

"What's A. A.?" asked Mrs. Hicken suspiciously.

"It's my nickname for Ann Aurelia. Goes faster."

Mrs. Hicken looked uncertain. "Aren't there a lot of meetings you have to go to?" she asked. "And those clubs are always looking for people to do work."

"They have oodles of good things to eat at the meetings," put in Ann Aurelia quickly. "At least they did at Eastside. We got to have some one time when we sang on their program. All kinds of cookies and cakes."

"And they don't make them out of mixes," added

Dorothy. "My mother made a real coconut cake last year. All fuzzy with coconut. It took her most of the morning."

Mrs. Hicken showed more interest. "But I'm not really Ann Aurelia's mother."

"That doesn't matter," said Dorothy. "There were two grandmas in it last year. And most of the teachers aren't anybody's mother."

"I'll think about it," said Mrs. Hicken. "But that reminds me. I forgot sugar and bread. Will you two go back to the supermarket for me?"

Both girls nodded. Mrs. Hicken set down her bag and opened her purse. She fumbled through it and pulled out a crumpled dollar bill. "And get yourselves some candy bars or something. And be sure to bring back the change. Don't lose it."

"We won't," promised Ann Aurelia.

"Thank you, ma'am," said Dorothy. "I like nut bars."

The two girls went skipping along the sidewalk, trying to avoid the cracks. But Ann Aurelia lost interest and stepped squarely on one.

"Dorothy," she said, "you won't tell the kids at school that Mrs. Hicken isn't my real mother, will you?"

"Okay. If that's what you want." Dorothy looked puzzled. "But you've got a different name."

"That won't matter. Milly Smith at the Home had a

mother who got married three times, and she had two different kinds of brothers and sisters. They were all there together. They didn't stay long though, because their mother just left them there to go to the hospital and have another baby."

"You don't say! Seems if she had that many different kinds of children, some of them could have baby-sat while she had the new one. Hughie took care of me and Shirley when Mama went to the hospital for Louise. We sure were glad to get Mama back because Hughie was an awful crank. He didn't get to play baseball for a whole week. And you should have tasted what he cooked up for us. I was only a little kid then, but I can still remember how fierce it was. All burnt—the pans too."

"But she came back."

"I don't mean to be nosey, A. A., but whatever did happen to your mother?"

"You're not nosey, Dorothy, and that's why I don't mind telling you things I wouldn't tell anybody else. Mr. Lacey took Mum away from me. He pretended at first that he liked me, but I could see through him all the time. Then when they got married, he didn't want me."

"He sounds like a real villain to me," said Dorothy. "I don't know him, but I don't like him."

Ann Aurelia tossed her head. "But if she likes Mr.

Lacey better than me, it's okay with me. She writes letters to me sometimes, but I don't even read them."

"Why not?"

"I don't want to hear about what she and Mr. Lacey are doing."

"Maybe she'll come back for you sometime," suggested Dorothy.

Ann Aurelia shook her head. "I'll never go to live with that Mr. Lacey. I've got Mrs. Hicken now. I like her and she likes me, so I don't need a mother anymore."

They continued on without stopping until they came to some scrawling on the sidewalk. Someone had written "Mickey loves Donna," and someone else, probably Mickey, had scratched lines across it and printed below in larger letters "HE DOES NOT."

"Who are Mickey and Donna?" asked Ann Aurelia.

"They're two silly kids at school. Mickey has a crush on her so he's always throwing things at her. They must be getting ready for school—writing stuff on the sidewalk already."

"Do any of the boys throw things at you?"

Dorothy shook her head vigorously. "They might break my glasses."

They soon reached the supermarket. It was the liveliest place in that part of town. The glass doors that opened and closed as if by invisible hands were swinging back and forth. Women carrying great bags of groceries were coming out. More were entering. Dogs scampered about hopefully.

Ann Aurelia and Dorothy followed a woman in slacks whose hair was up on huge pink rollers.

"Let's get a cart," said Ann Aurelia. "I like to push them around."

They tried out the carts.

"This one is all right," said Dorothy. "Its wheels don't go crooked."

Together they pushed it into the first aisle.

"Wouldn't it be fun if we had our own house and could buy all the things we wanted," said Dorothy. "What would you put in the cart?"

"Ice cream and pies and olives with red insides and—"

Dorothy had a sudden inspiration. "Say, why don't we play we have our own house together, and fill up this basket with what we'd buy."

"Oh, Mrs. Hicken didn't give me enough money for that, and I wouldn't dare anyhow."

"But we'll put it all back on the shelves after we've finished playing."

"Great!" exclaimed Ann Aurelia. "That will be more fun than Old Maid."

"Here's a can of peaches to begin with," said Dorothy, taking the can from the shelf. "The picture's so big I can tell without my glasses. Has it got extra heavy syrup?"

"Yep, it has. And pineapple. We want some of that for breakfast."

"But no prunes. *Glap!*"

"Maybe we should get them for our children," suggested Ann Aurelia. "Let's play that we have children at home."

"That's an idea. And why don't we go over there and look at the baby food."

They pushed past a woman who couldn't make up her mind between tomato juice and cranberry cocktail.

"Let's get some custard and mashed fruit," said Ann Aurelia. "*Oops!* We don't want any of this vegetable stuff. It looks worse than that drink we made."

"Long as we're down near the meat counter, let's go get hamburger and hot dogs. Our baby likes them better than this mushy stuff."

They loaded wieners, chopped meat, and salami into the cart.

"The pickles and things are down this next aisle," said Ann Aurelia. "Our children will need them with the hot dogs and hamburger. Oh, and olives too!"

"We'll need catsup," Dorothy reminded her. "And dill

pickles, and let's try this jar of red stuff."

"It says 'hot pepper relish,' " said Ann Aurelia, reading the label. "That will be good with anything."

At the frozen-food counter, they had a hard time making up their minds about the ice cream.

"Do you see fudge twirl or chocolate ripple down there," asked Dorothy, "or is there something that sounds better?"

"Why don't we take both?" asked Ann Aurelia. "It isn't costing us anything."

She dug into the stacks.

"Since that's the way it is," said Dorothy, "get some vanilla pecan and tutti-frutti."

Ann Aurelia also added a package of black cherry.

"My fingers are getting cold," she complained, "and we haven't got our candy bars yet. Let's go and get them now. They're way down at the other end. We can park our cart by that one over there so it'll be out of the way."

They headed for the other side of the market, running the gauntlet of slow-moving shoppers, carts parked in the middle of aisles, groups of gossiping women who hadn't seen each other since the day before, and a sniffing dog that had followed someone through the magic door.

This was the most difficult selection because it would be final. Ann Aurelia fingered a caramel bar and one

stuffed with marshmallow in turn. Dorothy couldn't decide between a chocolate bar with almonds and a larger one of solid peanuts.

"Maybe I'll take the peanut one," she finally decided. "It'll take longer to eat."

"I can hardly wait to eat mine," said Ann Aurelia, settling for the stuffed marshmallow. "Let's get our cart and put all that stuff back where it belongs. Then we'll get the sugar and bread and go home."

The girls went back to the ice-cream freezer.

There was only one cart near it.

"This isn't ours," said Dorothy. She lifted a cellophane package of parsnips gingerly. "We never would buy such stuff for our house."

"And soap chips!" exclaimed Ann Aurelia in disgust. "We wouldn't waste our money on that."

"But what's happened to our cart? I could swear we left it here."

"Maybe somebody pushed it somewhere else to get it out of the way."

"We'll just have to look for it," sighed Dorothy. "You go around the front, and I'll take the back. It's got to be somewhere in the store."

They parted company for the search. As Ann Aurelia came around the bread shelves, she spied the missing cart. An old lady had pushed it up to the check-out counter. She had already placed some of the items on the roller, and the clerk had begun checking them. But there was a puzzled look on the elderly woman's face as she stood staring through her glasses at the jar of hot pepper relish.

Ann Aurelia rushed up to her.

"Please, lady," she cried, "that's our cart."

The woman looked confused. She laughed with embarrassment. "Oh, excuse me. I'm so absent-minded. It was all the ice cream that fooled me. I always buy a lot because I love it. But you're lucky because now you can go right through."

She set the jar of relish on the counter. It went rolling up to the check-out girl—slowly but surely. The price blinked in the window of the cash register.

Ann Aurelia stood dumb with horror as the woman in slacks and with her hair in rollers pushed her cart into line.

She began impatiently unloading Ann Aurelia's things onto the moving counter. "Don't just stand there, little boy. I'm in a hurry. Left something cooking on the stove at home. Come! I'll help you."

Ann Aurelia was a picture in slow-motion as she laid her candy bar on the roller. She looked around frantically for Dorothy. The numbers in the register jumped up and down as the check-out girl punched the keys. Ann Aurelia tried to add them in her head, but they came and went too fast.

Then Dorothy came running up to the line. "What're you doing here, A. A.? Let's not go on playing this far."

The check-out girl tore a long numbered slip from the cash register. "Thirteen dollars and three cents," she pronounced, like a judge giving sentence.

Ann Aurelia looked at her in despair. "I've only got—a dollar."

Although she didn't know what Ann Aurelia was up to, Dorothy sensed that her playmate had been caught in some kind of a trap.

"Her mother forgot to give her the rest," she quickly told the girl. "We'll go right home and get it."

"I'll bag your order and set it aside for you," said the girl. "But you better get a move on before all this ice cream melts."

Ann Aurelia and Dorothy moved fast. They rushed to the door so quickly that it barely opened in time. They scrambled through, followed by the stray dog being chased out by a vigilant clerk. They raced through the parking lot, narrowly avoiding cars backing out and cars looking for spaces. They didn't stop until the supermarket was out of sight.

"I didn't mean to go through the line," panted Ann Aurelia. "That old lady already had our cart there. And the one behind was in such a hurry and kept putting our things on the counter to help me."

"That was a narrow escape."

"We won't go back there for a long time."

Ann Aurelia had a gloomy thought. "But we haven't got Mrs. Hicken's sugar and bread."

Dorothy had a gloomier one. "Nor our candy bars. I set mine on the magazine rack when I saw what was happening."

"And mine's in a bag at the counter."

"We'll go to some little store and get the sugar and bread," said Dorothy, brightening.

"And buy our candy bars there too," Ann Aurelia decided.

But as they walked down a side street, their steps grew slower and slower.

"It wouldn't be right to leave that girl with a lot of melted ice cream," said Ann Aurelia. "We better go home and tell Mrs. Hicken what happened."

"That's the best thing to do," agreed Dorothy.

IV

The Safety Patrol

That was nice of Mrs. Hicken to go down to the supermarket and pay for all that stuff we picked out," said Dorothy.

"I told you she's the greatest," declared Ann Aurelia. "She once said that getting mad just gets you tired out and doesn't do any good. That ice cream was awful sloppy, but once we put it in the freeze it stiffened up. And it was mighty nice of your mother to buy the fudge twirl and chocolate ripple and all the baby food from Mrs. Hicken."

"She's going to make bread pudding out of the baby food," said Dorothy. "She said she felt responsible since I was in it too. But getting mad doesn't make her tired out. She gave me the dickens. Daddy, too, because he hates bread pudding."

"But it gave your mother and Mrs. Hicken a good chance to get acquainted when they got together about the thing."

"And it looks like Mama has talked her into joining the P.T.A."

"They'll get to know each other even better then."

"It's a good thing school will soon be starting," said Dorothy. "That'll help keep us out of trouble. I've got to be real good because I'm on the regular Safety Patrol this year."

Ann Aurelia looked at her with awe. "You are! At Eastside we had boy safeties, and they had to be in sixth grade."

"We have mostly girls at Jefferson, and they're in the fifth and sixth. I just trained for it last year."

"I wish I could be a safety," said Ann Aurelia wistfully. "And wear one of those belts with a badge. You have that, don't you?"

Dorothy nodded. "And it says 'patrolman' on it." Her face suddenly brightened. "Sa-ay! Maybe you could be on the Patrol. Cindy Lewis who trained with me won't be back this year. They'll need somebody in her place."

"How do I get on it?"

"You'll have to see Mr. Denning who teaches sixth grade. He used to be a Marine so he's got lots of snap."

41

"You think he'll take me?"

"I'll ask first day of school," promised Dorothy. "We don't really start working until the second day when things get running on schedule."

"Will I have to know anything special since I've never been a safety before?"

"First you've got to have responsibility," Dorothy advised her. "Mr. Denning says that's the main thing. And you can't drop down in your marks. And you have to be on time every day."

"I will!" Ann Aurelia said.

"Me too. It's a serious job. Just like being a policeman. And you must have good judgment. That's what Mr. Denning says. You mustn't suddenly jump out in front of the cars with your flag. Wait until there's a hole in the traffic."

"That ought to be easy. You'll tell him I've got good judgment and responsibility, won't you, Dorothy?"

"Oh, I will! We both have."

"And I've always had good marks in school."

Dorothy kept her word. She came by Mrs. Hicken's house early on the first day of school so that they would have time to see Mr. Denning before the classes assembled.

"Why, A. A.," she declared, "I wouldn't have known you if it weren't for your head. I've never seen you in a dress! You almost look like a girl."

Ann Aurelia twirled the skirt of the candy-striped dress. "Mrs. Hicken helped pick it out. That's a pretty dress you have on, Dorothy, but you don't look any different except you've got your glasses back."

"We better hustle if we want to see Mr. Denning. Teachers are so busy first day. I don't see why. It's only half a day, and they usually don't even teach lessons."

Hand-in-hand they hurried down the street. Along the way they met other children who were going back to school. Dorothy knew two of them.

"Hi, Linda," she called gaily to a girl with long curly hair. She turned to Ann Aurelia. "This is Linda Spencer. She had a lot of warts on her hand last year. Still got some?"

Linda held up her hand. "No, I put white shoe polish on them, and they went away."

"Where'd you ever learn about doing that?"

"I didn't learn it anywhere," said Linda proudly. "I was just polishing my shoes for Sunday School, and I got the idea."

"That was real smart of you," said Dorothy. "It's like something A. A. and I would think of, wouldn't we?"

"Yep," answered Ann Aurelia. "Only I would have used brown polish so they'd look like freckles."

They soon reached the school. It was a modern brick

building, with more windows than brick. Ann Aurelia and Dorothy left Linda on the playground while they went inside. The halls smelled of fresh paint and disinfectant.

Dorothy knew exactly where she was going, and Ann Aurelia followed. They were halted by a sudden handclapping from behind.

A thin woman with bluish-white hair and steel-rimmed glasses stood in an open doorway. "Do you girls have permission to come inside before the bell has rung?" she demanded.

"We're just going to see Mr. Denning about the Safety Patrol," explained Dorothy.

"Then go there directly and don't loiter in the halls," commanded the elderly woman.

The girls quickened their steps.

"That's Miss Wyckoff I told you about," whispered Dorothy.

"I thought so," said Ann Aurelia.

Dorothy stepped into a doorway near the end of the hall.

A young man with broad shoulders and heavy black eyebrows sat at a desk writing in a notebook.

"Good morning, Mr. Denning," Dorothy greeted him.

"Why, good morning, Dorothy," answered Mr. Denning, with a smile that showed white, even teeth. "I'm glad to see you back."

"I'm right glad to be back. This is my friend, Ann Aurelia Wilson. She wants to be on the Safety Patrol. She's very responsible. And she has good judgment."

Mr. Denning looked Ann Aurelia up and down. "Were you at Jefferson last year?"

"No, sir," answered Ann Aurelia. "I went to Eastside."

"We like to have pupils who are familiar with this school, or who have had former experience."

"She'll get familiar, fast," put in Dorothy hastily. "I'll show her everything."

"Our Patrol is made up for this year," said Mr. Denning. "Maybe next year."

"Oh, no, it isn't," declared Dorothy triumphantly. "Cindy Lewis moved away this summer."

"I didn't know that," said Mr. Denning. He looked at the mound of papers and notebooks on his desk. "Perhaps I should give Ann Aurelia a chance. You will be responsible for her, Dorothy."

"Oh, thank you, Mr. Denning," cried Ann Aurelia in ecstasy.

"Don't thank me yet," he said abruptly. "You are not a permanent member of the Patrol yet. You will only be on trial. But if you perform your duties with responsibility and good judgment, you will win your badge for the whole year."

"You will find no cause to regret your confidence in me, sir," added Ann Aurelia, remembering the speech she had heard in one of the movies she and Dorothy had attended with Mrs. Hicken. She had memorized it for just such an occasion.

As they turned to go, Mr. Denning said, "Be here promptly at eight thirty tomorrow to get your belts and flags. Eight thirty sharp—not eight thirty-one."

"We will," promised the girls in chorus.

By the time they had finished their business with Mr. Denning, the bell was clanging through the halls. Dorothy took Ann Aurelia by the hand and led her toward the main door. She stopped and pointed. "Look! There they are behind the door."

A row of furled flags leaned against the wall. Clusters of glowing orange shoulder-belts hung from pegs.

Ann Aurelia went over and touched a flag reverently. She rubbed her hand lightly along a belt.

A sharp voice arrested them. "What did I say about loitering in the halls?"

They scrambled through the open door.

Ann Aurelia thought that her new school was wonderful. Fifth grade was wonderful. But most wonderful was the fact that she and Dorothy could have desks together.

First Miss Bennett briefly welcomed the children. She was a pretty young girl with a ready smile and a soft voice. She called the roll to see that everyone on her list was present.

"Since all of you are new to me," she announced, "at least new to my classroom, I would like to have each of you write his autobiography for me."

A redheaded boy in front of Dorothy raised his hand. "What's a autobiography?"

"Can anyone define *an* autobiography for Michael?" asked the teacher.

Several hands shot up, but Ann Aurelia's waved the most wildly.

"All right, Ann—Ann—"

"Aurelia. An autobiography is all about you and your life and what you do. We had to write one last year at Eastside."

"Very good, Ann Aurelia."

As soon as she had pencil and paper, Ann Aurelia wrote:

> My name is Ann Aurelia Wilson and I live at 122 Second Street. I have short hair and a plesent face. I am going to be on the Safety Patrol with Dorothy Grant. She is my best friend and we have oodles of fun together.

She frowned and looked around the room. She stared at her new teacher, who was busy writing in a big ledger. With her fluffy blonde hair, Miss Bennett really looked like a movie star.

Ann Aurelia put her pencil back to the paper.

> My mother is a famus movie star. She cant be with me all the time. She has gone to Hollywood to make a big picture so now I have to live with Mrs. Hicken.

She stopped writing and chewed the eraser on her pencil. She wondered what Mum was really doing. The first day of school she used to meet Ann Aurelia halfway when it was out so she could hear all about the new room and teacher. Probably today she was going to meet Mr. Lacey at his job and have lunch with him.

Ann Aurelia began writing again.

> When my mother comes back, well live in a big beautiful manshun and she will buy me silk dresses and jools like the pin full of real emeralds that she sent me for Christmas. We will live happily ever after.

Most of the others were still writing. Ann Aurelia looked dreamily out of the window. Then she carefully folded the paper when a boy came to collect it.

After that, time seemed to go fast. She could hardly believe that the final bell was ringing.

Dorothy didn't waste any time in coaching her for the duties of the Safety Patrol. She pointed to the crossing in front of the main door.

"We gather them here," she said. "Then when I tell you, you step out and hold up your flag so the cars have to stop. I'll go on leading the kids up the street, and you follow at the tail so there won't be any *loitering*—like Miss Wyckoff says. It's a long block up to Main Street, and we have to keep them moving. And don't let them get off the sidewalk."

"That sounds easy enough," said Ann Aurelia.

"It just sounds that way. See that wire fence up ahead? There are two yappy little dogs that run up and bark at the kids. Don't let any of them stop to poke their fingers through. Keep them moving from behind."

When they reached the fence, two watchful little terriers bounded to the wire and began barking ferociously. Ann Aurelia stopped to give each a pat on the nose.

"And don't do that when you're on Patrol," warned Dorothy.

It seemed to the girls a week instead of a day that they had to wait to begin their duties.

They were excused from class just before the last bell rang the next afternoon. They were both giddy with excitement. Dorothy showed Ann Aurelia how to buckle on the bright orange belt with its coveted badge. They proudly selected their flags and went outside.

Soon the other children were gathering on the sidewalk as class after class was dismissed.

"You wait and get them across this street," ordered Dorothy. "I'll go ahead and lead the line."

Ann Aurelia stood in the middle of the street and held her flag at arm's length as the children dashed past her to follow Dorothy. Her shoulders were pulled back so far that the buttons at her throat seemed ready to pop. She had made up her mind that an automobile would have to run over her before it could hit her charges.

Then the long straggling column of lively children started up the broad sidewalk on the other side. They chattered and shoved and waved their school papers. Dorothy fell into a stiff-legged goose step. She glanced over her shoulder as they began passing the barking terriers.

A few children paused briefly to look at them. Some made barking noises in response. Two bold boys pushed their fingers through the wire to see if the dogs really would bite.

"Stay away from that fence," bawled Dorothy, who was ready for this. "Haven't you ever seen dogs before? Step lively back there."

The dogs were left behind. But there was a new hurdle ahead. Workmen were digging a trench along the sewer line. Again Dorothy had to use her authority.

"That's nothing to gape at," she bawled. "Haven't you ever seen a hole in the ground? And you, Chuck Winters, get down off that dirt pile or I'll put you on report."

Some boys put their fingers to their noses and cried, *"Phew! Phew!"* As the last interested child looked down into the trench to see what was at the bottom, the column surged forward.

At its tail, Ann Aurelia had her own problems.

"Mickey Ryan, pick up that paper you just threw away. You want to grow up to be a litterbug and leave a mess everywhere you've been? You, boy in the blue sweater! Get back on the sidewalk and stop trying to run up ahead."

At last the column had safely crossed Main Street under the protection of Dorothy's flag. The children immediately broke ranks and went scurrying in different directions on their way home.

Dorothy gave a big sigh. "At least we got them here safe, A. A., and you did a super job for your first time."

"I just kept pushing them along," said Ann Aurelia modestly.

Things went smoothly on the following day. Ann Aurelia was sure that Mr. Denning would keep her on the Patrol. She worked hard at her lessons because she wanted to please Miss Bennett also.

She was delighted one day at recess time when Miss Bennett asked her to stay and help erase the blackboards. That was usually Geraldine Murphy's chore.

"Are you happy with Mrs. Hicken?" asked Miss Bennett.

Ann Aurelia was surprised. She wondered how the teacher knew about Mrs. Hicken. Then she remembered the autobiography which she had handed in.

"Oh, yes." She gave the blackboard an extra swipe. "She's the best. She's even joined the P.T.A. for me."

"Then you must always be loyal to her," said Miss Bennett. "People lose their own mothers in different ways. Mine died when I was a little girl, but I had a wonderful stepmother who raised me."

Ann Aurelia's face softened. "My Mum was wonderful to me too, before she went off to Hollywood. One time she took me to a carnival even though she had a chance to go to a swell dance. She'd even bought a special dress for it. But she took me to the carnival instead because I wanted to go so bad, and it was the last night."

"She sounds like a good mother. You must have had a lot of fun doing things together."

Ann Aurelia began to erase the blackboard with all her might.

"Mrs. Hicken is good to me too," she said defensively. "We have fun together. She takes me to movies and we watch TV shows together a lot."

It was over a week later, and Ann Aurelia and Dorothy had finished getting the children safely across Main Street. Ann Aurelia felt like a veteran now. She began twirling her flag as they slowly walked back to school.

"I'd like to be a drum majorette like you see in parades," she said.

She raised her knees high with each step and passed the stick from hand to hand.

"You look just like one," said Dorothy admiringly.

She followed suit. The girls circled in marching steps as they spun the flagsticks and passed them from hand to hand. Their backs were arched and their shoulders swayed as they pranced along.

"I saw a girl in the Fourth-of-July parade throw her silver stick way up in the air and catch it again," said Dorothy.

She gave hers a toss and missed it.

"Watch me," said Ann Aurelia. "Bet it goes as high as that girl you saw."

She squatted, then straightened suddenly as she tossed the flag upward. It fell to the ground.

"You almost did it," said Dorothy, "but we aren't supposed to play with the flags."

"Just one more try," said Ann Aurelia.

She made a lunge forward, putting all of her strength into sending the stick on its way. It shot up like an arrow. As it began its descent, the breeze carried it toward a tall chestnut tree. The yellow cloth snagged in a branch.

"Now you did it!" cried Dorothy.

The girls went under the tree and craned their necks. They tried to jump up and catch the branches.

"Here's a big stone," said Dorothy. "I'll try to hit the branch and then maybe the flag'll come loose."

She hurled the stone, but it only broke off a twig and then fell to the ground with a thud.

Ann Aurelia scanned the sidewalk for a better tool. "What about this stick. I'll throw it like a boomerang."

The stick spun into a crotch of the tree and remained there.

"It's up there really tight," groaned Ann Aurelia.

They anxiously studied the situation.

"If only we had a ladder," wished Dorothy.

"Or if only we could fly."

Dorothy finally admitted, "There's nothing left for us to do but go to Mr. Denning and tell him."

The head of the Safety Patrol glared at the two culprits cowering before his desk.

"Up in a tree!" he roared in his drill sergeant's voice. "How did a school safety flag get up in a tree?"

"I threw it up there," quavered Ann Aurelia. "I was playing I was a drum majorette."

He turned to Dorothy. "Didn't you teach her that the flags are not playthings?"

Dorothy nodded miserably. "But I was playing with mine too."

Mr. Denning looked at them sternly. "You will return your belts and badges to the hall. Both of you are hereby relieved of your duties on the Safety Patrol."

The girls walked slowly down the hall. They were ashamed and unhappy. They quickly unfastened their belts, and Dorothy set her flag in place. Ann Aurelia dusted off her badge with her cuff for the last time.

They plodded home dejectedly.

"I feel awful, Dorothy," said Ann Aurelia with a catch in her voice.

"Me, too," said Dorothy.

Ann Aurelia began to cry.

"Don't do that, A. A.," implored Dorothy. She tried to cheer her. "I'll tell you one thing. You threw that flagstick higher in the air than I ever saw *anybody* do in a parade."

V

The P.T.A. Meeting

Mrs. Hicken was flustered. She was getting ready for her first P.T.A. meeting.

"Which dress shall I wear, Ann Aurelia?" she asked anxiously. "What do they wear to the meetings?"

Ann Aurelia tried to remember. Neither Mrs. Jolly nor Mrs. Swann had ever been members.

"They just dress nice," she replied vaguely. "Why don't you wear your blue silk with the fringe?"

Mrs. Hicken looked desolate. "That dress has those spaghetti spots on it. I've been meaning to take it to the cleaners for a long time."

"What about the lavender that has ruffles on the skirt?"

"The cleaners must have shrunk it. I can't breathe when it's zipped up."

"Your cotton dress with the pink roses is pretty. Miss Wyckoff wore a dress like that one day, and it even looked good on her."

Mrs. Hicken was uncertain. "It's a drip-dry but the trouble is it dripped better than it dried. Needs a touch of the iron and I don't have time."

"I'll iron it for you while you're fixing your face," offered Ann Aurelia. "Mum always did more about her face than her clothes. She put on a lot of extra powder and rouge so the other ladies would think she looked too young to have a child in school."

"I've had my face too long to try to change it now," said Mrs. Hicken with a sigh. "I'll have to think most about my dress. I'll really be obliged to you if you'd iron it while I look for a clean handkerchief. I'm afraid they're all with the soiled clothes. I must get the washing done tomorrow for sure."

While ironing the flowered dress, Ann Aurelia discovered another casualty. "The hem's coming loose in back, Mrs. Hicken, and there isn't time to sew it now."

Mrs. Hicken was undaunted. "We'll fasten it with a safety pin. That's what I did with my winter skirt. Oh, dear! I must remember to fix it before the cold weather comes."

"I'll pin the hem for you," offered Ann Aurelia. "I'm

real neat when I want to be. Where are the safety pins?"

This time Mrs. Hicken was baffled. "There might be some in my top bureau drawer. But it's so cluttered we'd never be able to find them without emptying out everything. Perhaps there are a few in the sewing basket."

A search of the basket disclosed nothing but one straight pin.

"It will have to do," said Mrs. Hicken.

"Let me pin it up the best I can so that the point sticks outside. But you'll have to be careful when you sit down."

"Now if I can only find the mate to my other cotton glove. It's lost somewhere in the drawer too. But I always knew that Miss Watson wouldn't be looking in it—or the clothes hamper."

When Mrs. Hicken was fully attired, Ann Aurelia folded her arms and looked her over critically.

"You don't look too young," she admitted, "but you look like a mother. A lot of them at P.T.A. look like you."

Mrs. Hicken swelled with pride. "I just want you to be proud of me, Ann Aurelia."

"But I am. You look so honest and dependable. I bet they'll want you for president next year."

Mrs. Hicken looked not only honest and dependable

but frightened as well. "No, no! I told Mrs. Grant that I didn't want to be a very active member."

"Maybe you can say you're too busy," suggested Ann Aurelia. "Mum used to tell them that—or sometimes she'd say her health wasn't good."

"That's what I'll tell them. The doctor says I have too much weight for my age and that I should diet. But I won't put it that way. I'll say he told me I have to watch myself—that is, if they ask me to be president or something right off the bat."

After a few false starts out of the door, twice to look again for the missing glove and lastly to tell Ann Aurelia that there was almost half a peach pie and some liverwurst in the refrigerator if she wanted a snack at bedtime, Mrs. Hicken closed the front door firmly.

Ann Aurelia immediately made for the kitchen. Eating would pass the time until Mrs. Hicken's return. She wanted to stay awake for that.

When she opened the refrigerator door, she made a face at the gray liverwurst and pulled out the pie pan. She fizzed a can of whipped cream over the pie until it was covered with an avalanche. *Um-m-m!* Imagine having so much pie all to oneself!

Before she began on it, she went to her bedroom and pulled the latest comic book that Dorothy had lent her from the stack under the bed. Then she settled herself at the kitchen table and began reading "Octopus Man" while she ate the pie.

Octopus Man had tentacles instead of arms and legs. He could crawl on the ceiling or squeeze through transoms looking for his human prey. The only creatures who gave him any trouble were a man with the head of a tiger and his girl friend who had a green face and claws like a cat's.

"Silly people!" mumbled Ann Aurelia through a mouthful of whipped cream. There weren't any real people like that. Even Mum with her green eye shadow and long red fingernails hadn't looked as odd as the woman in the magazine. And she certainly hadn't gone on dates with freaks.

But Ann Aurelia read on eagerly, enjoying what her eyes were seeing and her teeth chewing.

The words in the comics were silly too. There were "YOOEEE's" and "EEEYAA's" in big capital letters. Who ever screamed like that? "C'mon" and "wanna!" Hadn't the people who drew the comics ever gone to school and learned to spell?

And the pictures looked as if they had been colored with crayons by first graders. But she and Dorothy liked the comics because they were exciting.

When she reached the end of the fantastic happenings and the peach pie, Ann Aurelia carefully wiped the flecks of whipped cream from the gaudy cover and then set the pie pan to soak until morning.

Her eyes were feeling squinty, but it wasn't yet time for Mrs. Hicken to return. Maybe she could get into bed and listen to the radio for awhile. That should make time pass fast.

Once in bed with her head on the soft pillow, the thing that makes time pass fastest happened to Ann Aurelia. She fell fast asleep.

She began to dream about the comics. The tiger-headed man had carried off Mum and thrown her into a crocodile pit. Ann Aurelia was battling the crocodiles to get to her mother when she suddenly remembered the space gun in her pocket. She shot all the crocodiles into nothingness and then ran to Mum. But slowly Mum's face turned green all over and her red fingernails grew into claws. She howled a horrible "GRRRORA" and pounced on Ann Aurelia. She began shaking her as if she were a mouse.

Ann Aurelia tried to scream for help, but no "YOOEEE's" or "EEEYAA's" would come from her throat.

At last a scream came out. But it wasn't the green-faced woman shaking her. It was Mrs. Hicken.

"What's wrong, Ann Aurelia?" she asked. "I didn't scare you, did I?"

When she realized that she had only been dreaming, Ann Aurelia giggled.

"Dreams are silly too," she said. Then she sat bolt upright. "What happened at the P.T.A.? Did they want to make you president or anything? Did you meet some nice ladies?"

Mrs. Hicken tried to be modest. "I'm to be hostess next month and appoint a committee to make the refreshments."

Ann Aurelia was now wide awake. "But you said you weren't going to do any work."

"It's not really much work," said Mrs. Hicken apologetically. "I just call people on the telephone and make sure the things for the coffee get there. Besides, the hostess and her committee get to bring home all the leftover goodies. Come out in the kitchen and see the big box I've brought—brownies and frosted cakes and even some gingerbread a new friend of mine brought."

"But you weren't hostess this time," Ann Aurelia pointed out.

"Mrs. Grant suggested they give me some of the leftovers since I volunteered for next month."

"You *volunteered?*"

"Not exactly," explained Mrs. Hicken. "They asked if

somebody would volunteer. I was thinking about it and how good the coffee was already smelling and what a lot of interesting bags and boxes some of those women had carried in. Guess I began wriggling around trying to make up my mind because just then I got an awful prick from that pin. It made me jump right up. Before I could do anything, I heard Mrs. Grant say, 'Thank you for volunteering, Mrs. Hicken. It's a pleasure to have a new member so eager to help.' "

Ann Aurelia was reassuring. "Oh, you won't be sorry, Mrs. Hicken. I bet you'll be the greatest hostess they ever had. But did you meet Miss Bennett and talk about my work?"

"Indeed I did. She says you're one of the bright ones in her class. Said she never had a pupil with so much imagination. She's the prettiest teacher there. Wonder if she bleaches her hair."

"She wouldn't do that," declared Ann Aurelia loyally. "She's real. She does wear lipstick—sort of pinkish—but everybody does."

"I don't," said Mrs. Hicken, "but perhaps I should. Maybe I'll buy a lipstick for when I'm hostess next month. And I'm going to get busy fixing up my clothes that need it. I never had anywhere much to wear them before."

VI

The Nature Walk

What do we do on a nature walk?" asked Ann Aurelia. "We never had one of those at Eastside."

"It's fun and we don't have to go to class in the morning," explained Dorothy. "We take a bag lunch to eat like a picnic. And we ride one of the school buses out to River Park and collect leaves for our science books."

"I've never been there. Mum was going to take me one time, but then she married Mr. Lacey. Is it pretty?"

"Lots of woods and a big river, but they won't let us near it. Anybody who does has to go back to the bus and sit there the rest of the time."

"Don't we even get to see it?"

"Sure, but we have to look down a big hill, and they keep telling us to stay away from it because we might fall in."

"I never fell in a river," said Ann Aurelia, "but one time I slipped in the bathtub and got my nose full of water."

"Hughie fell off his ship once and almost drowned. He'll be coming home soon."

"When?"

"We don't know for sure. He likes to surprise us. But I think it'll be next month. Hughie's lots of fun and likes to play jokes."

It turned out that the nature walk was as Dorothy had described it. The fifth and sixth grades gathered impatiently on the playground to await the arrival of the bus.

"Look!" groaned Dorothy. "It's Miss Wyckoff going with us this time. Isn't that just our luck?"

They watched Miss Wyckoff come down the steps with a brisk, measured step. She wore a gray tweed coat, a loose black turban, and very sensible shoes. She clapped her hands sharply.

"Line up, boys and girls. The bus is coming now. No shoving or other disorder will be permitted."

The pupils gathered into a solid group that slowly lengthened into two lines. They gripped their lunch bags tightly. They scuffled for good places.

"Hurry! Hurry!" ordered Miss Wyckoff. "Don't waste

66

time. Time is one of our most precious commodities. Michael and Charles, what seems to be the trouble?"

"He's pushing me," accused Chuck.

"I am not," declared Mickey. "He won't step back and he keeps breathing down my neck."

Miss Wyckoff separated them with a sweep of her arm. "No pushing, Michael. No breathing, Charles. Forward march. Chins up. Enter the bus and take your seats in an orderly manner."

The lines surged forward, slowed at the bus door, then scattered as the children scrambled for seats with their favorite classmates.

Ann Aurelia and Dorothy quickly picked out places near the front where they could see more. To their disappointment, Miss Wyckoff seated herself directly in front of them, her turban blocking their view.

"I hoped Miss Bennett would come with us," Dorothy whispered.

"Me, too," said Ann Aurelia. "She's probably stuck with Miss Wyckoff's room now."

"I bet it's because Miss Wyckoff is better at making us behave," Dorothy whispered again.

The bus couldn't leave immediately. The children craned their necks to discover the cause for the delay. It turned out that they were waiting for Mr. Thornton, the principal, who would follow the bus in his own car.

The bus driver sat slouched over the wheel as if he didn't care if they ever started. His lips turned down at the corners like Miss Wyckoff's. But his eyes, unlike her sharp ones, were sad and brooding. His voice had a tired hoarseness. He had been driving school buses for many years.

At last he grudgingly turned on the ignition. The bus jiggled. The seats vibrated. There was a lurch forward, and the bus began rattling down the street.

For several blocks the children were silent. Then a low buzz filled the bus. It grew louder. It rose to a pitch and the children had to yell to be heard.

The bus driver ignored it all as if his ears had been completely deafened long before. But Miss Wyckoff rose from her seat and turned in the aisle.

"Stop this bedlam immediately," she commanded, "or we shall return to our classrooms."

The din halted in mid-air. The rest of the ride was made in human silence but mechanical racket because the bus was very old.

At last they reached the park. It was on a wooded slope with deserted picnic tables in a clearing. The trees were gay with red and yellow leaves.

The pupils eagerly scraped out of their seats and began

scrambling into the aisle. Before they could reach the exit, Miss Wyckoff had another command.

"You are positively forbidden to go over the hill to the river," she said. "We don't want any pupils to be drowned." She pursed her lips to show that this was final.

They again had to wait for Mr. Thornton's car before they began the walk. Then the children were lined up with Miss Wyckoff in the lead. The principal brought up the rear so that there would be no stragglers to get lost.

Miss Wyckoff acted as guide. "You will note that these trees on our right are sugar maple. You can usually identify them by their beautiful scarlet leaves. The birches, on the other hand, are quite yellow."

Some of the children began breaking off branches.

"No, no," forbade Miss Wyckoff. "We must not damage the trees. Gather the leaves that have already fallen."

The children threw the branches away as if they were on fire. They stooped here and there to pick up the most colorful specimens on the ground.

"Look!" cried Mickey, pointing up to the sky. "Birds! You can hear them too."

"Wild geese migrating to the south," Miss Wyckoff informed them. "We are extremely lucky to see such a sight."

The geese made a dark gray wishbone in the light gray

sky. The sad whine of their farewell song drifted to the children below. Some of the boys began flapping their arms to show off.

"Take me with you," cried Mickey, who was the biggest showoff. "I want to go south too. Can I go south, Miss Wyckoff?"

"*May* I go south," the teacher corrected him. "You may not go south and you cannot go south. Don't act silly, Michael."

"There's the river down there!" exclaimed Dorothy.

"It shines so pretty through the trees," said Ann Aurelia. "And what are those things like witches' brooms on that old dead tree over the water?"

Miss Wyckoff looked excited herself.

"Mistletoe!" she answered joyously. "Now there is a splendid sight. I didn't know it grew in this park. It would be nice to get some for the science class." She started forward, then caught herself. "But we must not go near the river. Someone might fall in."

She seemed to be disciplining herself as well as the children when she turned around with determination. "Come! Come! We must return. It will be lunch time when we get back."

The pupils kept looking back wistfully at the source of Miss Wyckoff's temptation. The green clumps of mistletoe hung tantalizingly low just a few feet out over the water.

Once back at the picnic tables, they tore into their lunch bags like squirrels breaking nuts. The food went down much faster than was usual in the school cafeteria.

"Mr. Thornton," said Miss Wyckoff as the children gathered the rubbish and carried it to nearby cans, "I should like to go back and gather some of the mistletoe for science. With your permission, I will take two dependable pupils with me to help carry it back. I will be responsible for their safety."

"Me, me," cried a chorus of voices. "I'll help pick it too."

Miss Wyckoff clapped her hands for silence. "We do not have Mr. Thornton's permission yet," she admonished them.

"Indeed you have," the principal said. "I know any child will be safe with you, Miss Wyckoff."

"I will select Dorothy Grant," stated the teacher. "She may choose her companion."

So Miss Wyckoff started back over the trail again with Dorothy and Ann Aurelia in her wake. A delicious feeling came over the girls as they drew closer and closer to the forbidden river. They followed its shine through the leaves to its full glory as it swept along the steep bank.

"Careful now, girls," warned Miss Wyckoff as they edged their way down. "Don't come any farther. The bank goes straight down, and the water is quite deep here. I wouldn't want either of you to fall in."

The mistletoe seemed higher and farther from the shore now.

"Maybe I can get a stick for us to pull it in," suggested Dorothy.

"I could climb the tree and push that branch down," offered Ann Aurelia.

"Indeed not!" said Miss Wyckoff. "That would be dangerous. Here! I think I can reach for it. I have long arms."

She dug her heels into the bank. She cautiously stretched a long arm toward the green clump. But the mistletoe eluded her grasp.

"I think I've got it. Yes, I've almost reached it. If I can only make my arm longer."

There was a grating of pebbles under her sensible shoes as she lost her balance. There was a big splash as she dropped into the river.

Dorothy screamed. Ann Aurelia stared down with horror as Miss Wyckoff's arms thrashed the water.

"Help! Help!" blubbered Miss Wyckoff, her coat and

skirt rising around her now hatless head.

"I can't swim, Miss Wyckoff," cried Dorothy despairingly.

"Me neither," cried Ann Aurelia.

As Miss Wyckoff's white head went under, the girls looked around frantically for a stick or a piece of rope.

"This big bush," panted Dorothy. "We'll bend a branch down so she can catch hold."

She was already pushing against the bush. Ann Aurelia feverishly joined her. They panted and perspired as they tried to bend a strong branch down to the water. Then Dorothy's feet slipped from under her. She would have fallen into the water too if it hadn't been for her strong grip on the bush, but the weight of her body successfully lowered the branch to Miss Wyckoff's reach.

"Grab hold, Miss Wyckoff," shouted Ann Aurelia as the woman's head broke water again. "Grab that branch right there. It's close now."

Miss Wyckoff's long arm shot toward the bush. Her hand gripped the end of a branch tightly. She pulled her other arm from the river. Her fingers closed on some of the twigs. Then Ann Aurelia grasped Dorothy's wrist and helped to pull her up the bank again.

"I'll go get Mr. Thornton," panted Ann Aurelia. "You stay and watch Miss Wyckoff."

A shower of dirt fell into the water as Ann Aurelia's feet scraped hastily up the bank. She went bounding along the trail like a rabbit flushed by hounds.

"It's all right now." Dorothy tried to encourage Miss Wyckoff. "There'll be help here in no time. Just hang on tight."

For some minutes, the teacher clung to the bush with a death grip. Dorothy anxiously peered through the trees. From time to time she cried, "Help, help!"

"I—I'm getting a little tired," said Miss Wyckoff.

"No, you aren't," said Dorothy. "You can't. I'll recite something for you. I'll recite Mark Anthony's speech like you taught us last year. 'Friends, Romans, countrymen, lend me your ears.'" She turned and shouted, "Help, help" through the woods because she could see that Miss Wyckoff's grasp was weakening. "'I come to bury Caesar not to praise him.' Help, help! I can't remember the rest."

"'The evil—that—men—do,'" murmured Miss Wyckoff through blue lips.

"Save your breath, Miss Wyckoff. I'll say the tables for you instead. I'll say the twelves. Twelve times one is twelve. Twelve times two is twenty-four. Twelve times three is thirty-eight."

"No, Dorothy," corrected Miss Wyckoff. "Twelve times—three—is thirty-six. I can't—hold—on—any longer."

"Don't say 'I can't,' Miss Wyckoff. Remember you always told us that, when we said we couldn't do something. You said there's no such word as 'can't.' And we finally did it. You can hold on till help comes."

"I'll try," promised Miss Wyckoff faintly.

"Twelve times four is—here they come! Here comes Mr. Thornton and Mr. Trickett!"

The two men raced down the bank, followed by Ann Aurelia.

"You still got Miss Wyckoff on the bush?" she cried.

"Yes," said Dorothy in relief. "It took some arithmetic."

"Grab that tree, Horace, and hold onto my hand tightly," ordered Mr. Thornton. "I can reach for her."

The men made two links in a human chain as Mr. Thornton hung over the bank. He gripped Miss Wyckoff's cold white wrist and pulled with all his might. The teacher rose from the river like a great hooked fish. Rivulets from her soaked clothing ran down the bank.

"I've got her," Mr. Thornton told the driver. "I'll carry her back and take her to the doctor in my car. You gather the children together and drive them back to school."

The driver drearily nodded. "I've never seen it to fail on these trips," he muttered. "Last year it was the kids into poison ivy, and the year before that the skunk."

Even though Miss Wyckoff wasn't present, the ride back was as orderly as she would have wished. The children were overawed by the terrible accident that had befallen her. They talked together in low tones, as if they were sitting outside a death chamber.

"She was a good teacher," said Mickey. "I learned a lot in her class even if she was cranky."

"One time I lost my lunch money; she loaned me forty cents of her own," said Donna, remembering.

"She kept a real neat desk," put in Chuck, "and she never sent us to Mr. Thornton. She punished us herself."

No one could remember anything but good of Miss Wyckoff.

"It's like that speech I was reciting to keep her hanging on," said Dorothy. "The good men do lives after them and the evil is interred within their bones—or maybe it's the other way around. Miss Wyckoff would know."

"It's too bad we don't know how to swim," said Ann Aurelia. "We could have saved her life."

To their surprise, Miss Wyckoff appeared at school the next morning. She seemed quite her old self. She scolded Dorothy and Ann Aurelia for running in the hall, and made no mention of what had happened on the nature walk.

"A special assembly has been called for eleven o'clock,"

Miss Bennett told her class, "so we will not have social studies at that time."

Mr. Thornton opened the assembly by clearing his throat as he always did when he had an important announcement to make.

"We are gathered here to honor two pupils whose presence of mind and quick action helped to save a teacher's life," he stated. "Dorothy Grant and Ann Aurelia Wilson, please step up on this platform."

The girls were so stunned that for a few moments they made no move. Then Dorothy plucked at Ann Aurelia's arm. "He must mean us," she whispered.

Self-consciously they climbed the steps to the platform and faced Mr. Thornton. Dorothy twisted her fingers nervously. Ann Aurelia rocked from one foot to the other. Their faces grew hotter and hotter as the principal explained to the whole school their part in saving Miss Wyckoff from drowning.

Mr. Thornton ended his speech by calling into the wings: "Mr. Denning, we are ready now."

The sixth-grade teacher marched across the stage. In one hand he held two Safety Patrol flags. In the other were the matching belts.

He handed a flag to each girl. Then with great ceremony, he buckled a belt on each. He stepped back, clicked his heels, and saluted with military snap.

"For unfailing courage in the face of extreme danger," he announced, "you are hereby reinstated as members of the Jefferson Safety Patrol."

The whole assembly broke into cheers, and some of the boys whistled shrilly.

VII

Hallowe'en

Hallowe'en's coming," said Dorothy, as she and Ann Aurelia walked home from school a few weeks later. "Next to Christmas, I like it best."

"Me too," agreed Ann Aurelia. "It's more exciting than Christmas. And nobody expects you to be good."

"Only trouble is I have to take Louise trick-or-treating every Hallowe'en. Makes you feel like a little kid yourself."

"Mum used to take me out when I was little. Then we'd go home and eat the candy together and laugh about the people. We'll be going out this Hallowe'en together, won't we?"

"Sure will."

"Mrs. Hicken's been saving little scraps of soap for me for ages. She said just not to soap up her windows, or any of the neighbors. I'll have to go off where we don't know anybody."

"Have you got a costume to wear? I have a witch hat and cape from last year."

"Mrs. Swann gave me a torn sheet last year so I could be a ghost. But I've never had a real costume since I lived with Mum. She sewed me the prettiest gypsy dress with a flowered skirt, and she let me wear her long earrings and all her clanky bracelets."

"Sounds like you miss your mother," said Dorothy.

"No, I don't," retorted Ann Aurelia. "I don't need anybody. Nobody but you and Mrs. Hicken. Anyway, I guess Mr. Lacey needed her worse. Maybe Mrs. Hicken would make me a costume. No! She doesn't like to sew. Says it wastes time when she could be watching TV. But maybe she'd let me buy one with some of the money Miss Watson gives her."

"I've got a big idea, A. A.! Why don't we two make you a costume. I can sew a little."

"Great! We'll make a real different one so nobody will know me."

"Different like those sandwiches we made at Mrs. Hicken's yesterday with the sliced onions and blackberry jam," said Dorothy. "Mama's got a whole pillowcase full of sewing scraps."

"Remember those puppets we made out of bags at school, when I made a little monster? Let's us make me a great big monster head for a mask."

"With long sharp teeth," said Dorothy.

"And hairy eyebrows."

"We'll need a big grocery bag."

But when the girls reached the Grant house and began searching the kitchen closets, Dorothy saw something even better. "This big carton with the soup cans in it—it will make you have a square head, and we can cut better teeth."

The girls went into a flurry of work. Dorothy found the kitchen scissors and sent Louise for the scrapbag in their mother's dress closet.

"I remember there are some fur pieces from an old coat she had one time. She was going to sew them on a winter dress for Shirley, but they'll be better on the monster. First we've got to make his ugly face. I'll start cutting out the mouth and the teeth."

She began jabbing at the carton with the scissor points.

"That cardboard's hard, isn't it?" asked Ann Aurelia anxiously.

"Maybe the butcher knife would work better." Dorothy opened a drawer and took out a shiny, broad-bladed knife. "Stand way back, A. A., so I don't cut you."

She worked with her brow wrinkled and the tip of her tongue held tightly between her teeth. She succeeded in making a jagged curve in the carton. "I can't make teeth while I'm doing this. We'll cut them out separate and paste them in. I'll try—ouch!" She dropped the knife and quickly put her finger into her mouth.

"Did you cut yourself?" asked Ann Aurelia anxiously.

Dorothy held the finger out. "I know what," she cried. "We'll smear the blood all over the monster's mouth. That really will look fierce. Isn't it lucky I cut my finger?"

She rubbed her fingertip back and forth across the jagged edge of cardboard until the flow of blood stopped.

"We haven't got enough on yet," she complained. She pinched her finger. "But maybe I can squeeze out a couple more drops."

Louise returned, dragging the pillowcase behind her. Her face was almost hidden under a hat covered with pink roses.

Dorothy was dismayed. "Louise, you take Mama's hat off and put it back in the closet."

"I want a monster head," protested Louise.

"You know Mama would give you a licking if she saw you. She already bought you that Mickey Mouse costume. You take her hat right back or I'll tell."

But Louise was too interested in the monster head to

move. She pointed her finger at the pink smear on the cardboard.

"Catsup," she said.

"That's it!" exclaimed Ann Aurelia. "Let's smear a lot of catsup on it. That blood just looks pink anyhow."

"Louise," Dorothy complimented her little sister, "you're a smart little kid. You take after your big sister Dorothy sometimes. Now put that hat back and I won't tell Mama on you."

Louise solemnly nodded her head and left.

When the face was finished to their satisfaction— although Ann Aurelia complained that the eyes were too far apart for her to see through them—the girls began digging into the pillowcase.

"We'll paste these pieces of fur over the rest of the carton, and maybe have some rags hanging down," said Dorothy.

At last they stood back and critically studied the finished product.

"It's the ugliest thing I ever saw," admitted Dorothy proudly.

"Do you think it will scare everybody?" asked Ann Aurelia. "I won't really need any other costume. I'll just wear my slacks so I can run faster."

"We'll find out if it's scarey enough. Let's try it on Louise."

Dorothy called her little sister. A clomping sound answered her. Louise limped in wearing her mother's high-heeled shoes.

"What's the matter with you?" said Dorothy angrily. "You stay out of Mama's closet and take off those shoes. I'll carry them back."

"Isn't this a fierce monster, Louise?" asked Ann Aurelia, pretending great fright. "Look at his teeth all ready to bite you, and his shaggy old head."

Louise stepped out of the shoes. She went to the carton and gave it a slap.

"I'll put it on my head," decided Ann Aurelia. "Maybe it will seem more real then." She lowered the carton over her short hair until it rested on her shoulders. "I can't see out of one eye, and it sure smells like catsup. *Gr-r-r!* I'm going to eat you up, Louise. *Gr-r-r! Gr-r-r!*"

The little girl gave a shriek and made for the living room. Her screams were muffled as she crawled behind the couch.

"I want A. A. back," she bawled. "Where's A. A.?"

"There!" exclaimed Dorothy. "We've got an extra-special super monster."

Ann Aurelia lifted the carton from her head. "It's all right, Louise. It's just me. Come on out."

Louise hesitated a few seconds. She crawled out slowly. She looked from the monster to Ann Aurelia's face. She strode to the monster and hit the carton with her fist. "Go away, monster!"

"We'll scare them good on Hallowe'en night," promised Ann Aurelia.

"If you don't want to wear it," said Dorothy, "you can go to windows and stick the head up. That will scare the people inside to death. Louise, quit punching the monster. You want to bust him up before Hallowe'en even gets here?"

The girls worked on the carton many afternoons before Hallowe'en finally arrived. Louise couldn't wait for night to come, so Dorothy and Ann Aurelia had to take her around while it was still light.

They set out with their big grocery bags. At most houses they were given handfuls of mixed candies. At one, a man came to the door and gave each of them a nickel. A woman who had forgotten it was Hallowe'en gave them a small jar of sweet pickles to share.

"It's time to go home now, Louise," said Dorothy. "You'll be sick if you get any more of this stuff."

But Louise was having too much fun to give up the game.

"It's getting dark, isn't it?" Dorothy called her little sister's attention to lights coming on in some windows. "It's getting real spooky out."

Ann Aurelia helped to change Louise's mind. "I bet a lot of real ghosts will be coming out now. Listen! Hear that creaky noise behind the hedge?"

"Maybe I'll go home now," Louise decided.

It was really dark by the time that they had left the little girl and the three bags safely inside the door.

The pale moon looked like the ghost of the earth. A wailing wind slowly rose. It chased the dead leaves across the pavements. The bare branches of trees clawed and clutched like skeleton fingers. It was just the kind of night for a witch and a monster to be abroad.

Ann Aurelia started out with the carton on her head. But it was hard to see through one hole at a time, and she tripped twice. She pulled off the monster head and carried it in her arms.

"When anybody comes, I'll put it back on," she told the witch at her side.

"Now we can really have fun," said Dorothy. "Let's ring some doorbells and run."

After ringing a few, Ann Aurelia brought out her bits of soap. They began scrawling on cars parked along the curb.

Soon they heard hoots and catcalls in the distance.

"It's the boys," said Dorothy. "They're coming this way."

"Let's hide behind this car and give them a big scare with the monster head."

They squatted behind the trunk of the automobile. The boys came closer. Dorothy peeped around a fender.

"They're squirting that foam stuff on the cars," she said. "Mickey Ryan's one of them. I can tell his voice."

The girls giggled. Ann Aurelia pulled the monster head over her own. The voices came closer.

"Let's cover this one good," said Mickey.

At that instant, Ann Aurelia gave a wild whoop and jumped out toward the boys. There was instant panic among them. Two screeched and they all took to their heels.

"We better get out of here fast," Dorothy warned the monster. "They're just surprised. They'll come back after us."

Already the boys were gathering under a pale street-light to muster their forces for the attack.

Ann Aurelia pulled the carton from her head, and both girls began running down the sidewalk. Immediately the boys followed in hot pursuit. Ann Aurelia dropped the monster head as she and Dorothy broke through a hedge to look for a hiding place.

A big dog lunged toward them, barking savagely. Dorothy yanked off her witch hat and threw it at him. As the dog stopped to tear the hat apart, the girls broke through the hedge again. They were now back on the sidewalk.

Fortunately the boys had stopped to examine the monster head lying in their path. This gave Ann Aurelia and Dorothy another head start.

They saw a strange man in a heavy overcoat walking toward them. Dorothy ran up to him and grabbed his arm.

"Please, mister," she panted, "may we be your children for just a little while?"

"Some boys are chasing us," explained Ann Aurelia breathlessly. "Will you hold our hands until we get past them?"

"No trouble at all," said the man. "I already have six children at home."

Each girl took a hand and pressed closer to him as they approached the enemies. The boys were taking turns stomping on the monster head. It was almost flattened, and pieces of fur littered the sidewalk.

The boys capered like demons. They chanted, "The monster's dead! The monster's dead! We've got his head! We've got his head!"

They hurled taunts at the girls and their protector as they passed. "Scat! Scat! Fraidy cat! Fraidy cat!" One daring boy ran up and squirted the white foam on Ann Aurelia.

When the trio reached the automobile that Ann Aurelia and Dorothy had soaped, the man said, "This is my car so I'll have to leave you now."

"Thank you for being our father," said Dorothy.

"Thanks a million," said Ann Aurelia.

"You're welcome," replied the man. "You'd better go straight home now."

They watched the automobile drive away.

"I'm sorry we soaped up his windows," said Dorothy.

"He was such a nice man," said Ann Aurelia. "I wish Mr. Lacey had been that nice."

"Too bad your mum didn't meet that man in the car first," said Dorothy. "Let's not soap any more cars. They might belong to nice people like him. Let's go home and eat our candy and pickles before Louise gets into them."

"It's no more fun now that they broke our monster."

"And it was such a beautiful monster."

As they approached her house, Dorothy clutched Ann Aurelia.

"Funny it's all dark," she quavered. "Mama always leaves the lights on inside and out on Hallowe'en night."

"It looks like everybody's gone," said Ann Aurelia. "Maybe they went out to a movie."

"Not on Hallowe'en night. Daddy doesn't want his car soaped up."

They slowly tiptoed toward the dark house. Each could feel the beating of her own heart. They held hands tightly as they crept toward the front door.

Suddenly they stopped! Was that a groan behind the hydrangea bush?

Yes, it was! It was growing louder. A white "thing" slowly rose from behind the bush. Before their terrified eyes, it grew as tall as the roof.

"It's coming after us," shrieked Dorothy.

They let go of hands and fled down the sidewalk. Ann Aurelia sprinted ahead, screaming wildly, "Help! Help! It's after us!"

The "thing" was gaining on them. It was closing in on Dorothy. With a sudden pounce, it seized her and muffled her screams. Her glasses slid to the sidewalk.

Ann Aurelia looked over her shoulder and saw what had happened. She frantically looked around for some kind of weapon. She would have to save Dorothy from the "thing" some way. She began to jerk at one of the pickets in the nearby fence.

Dorothy bit and kicked as she struggled in the folds of white cloth. Then a deep voice said in her ear, "What's the matter? Your old brother Hughie been gone so long you don't even know him when you see him?"

Dorothy squirmed around and hugged the "thing" tightly. She was half-crying with relief.

"Hughie!" she scolded in a shaky voice. "You've just scared us out of our skins. And you made me lose my glasses." She called over her shoulder, "It's all right, A. A. It's only Hughie in a sheet."

"And a broomstick," added her brother. "Needed that to lift the sheet high."

He picked up her glasses and handed them to her.

VIII

The Surprise Party

Your brother Hughie is oodles of fun," said Ann Aurelia as she and Dorothy walked to school the next Friday morning.

A light snow had fallen during the night, and their boots squeaked through it.

"He scared us silly on Hallowe'en, didn't he?" asked Dorothy appreciatively.

"Worse than that horror movie he took us to the last night of his leave. And when your mother didn't want us to go, he talked her into it."

"He loves horror movies himself. Says they make things in real life seem less bad."

"I wish he could have stayed longer," said Ann Aurelia wistfully. "Just when we were having so much fun with him, he had to go back to his ship."

It turned out to be a hard morning for the Safety Patrol. Boys stood in the middle of the street and threw snowballs. Girls slipped and fell. Everybody tried to delay going into the schoolhouse.

Miss Bennett smiled understandingly when some of them were tardy.

"I have to check the list and count the money for lunch milk," she announced, "so you'll have a spelling game while I'm busy. I believe it is Dorothy Grant's turn to read the words. Take out the speller, Dorothy, and turn to page twenty-seven. Read the first column, and give everyone time to write each word."

Miss Bennett's fluffy hair shone with hidden lights as she bowed over her desk to count change and check names. She busied herself, neatly stacking dimes, nickels, and pennies in tiny towers.

Then she raised her head. "When you are finished, pass your papers to the pupil behind, then Dorothy will slowly spell each word so that the papers may be corrected and marked."

Dorothy gave the correct spelling as pencils paused or scratched. When she had finished, she sat down and began to tidy the drawer of her desk. The papers were passed back to their owners.

Mickey Ryan scowled at his, then glared back at

Chuck Winters. His arm thrashed through the air.

"Yes, Michael," said Miss Bennett.

"He marked my paper a hundred percent, and I got two wrong," accused Mickey with disgust. He shoved the paper under Chuck's nose. "You're dumb."

"Now, boys and girls," said Miss Bennett, "we all make mistakes sometimes, and the mark does not count on your record. It is only a game. But be more careful after this, Charles. You will have a new teacher next semester. I want her to see that this class has good habits. When I am gone, I still want to be proud of you."

The eyes of the fifth-grade pupils were full of surprise and shock. Dorothy stared into her drawer. Ann Aurelia's lips trembled as she began doodling over her spelling paper.

The classroom was unusually orderly until the recess bell rang. It was as if the children couldn't wait to show off their good habits.

Because it was cold outside, they spent recess in the large school basement. Once there, the fifth-grade pupils gathered in a buzzing group.

"She said she's leaving," said Donna. "Why do you suppose?"

"Maybe Mr. Thornton's firing her," guessed Mickey.

"Perhaps because we're so bad," suggested Chuck.

"Why did you have to make all that trouble about your paper, Mickey? I don't see why you couldn't be satisfied with a hundred percent."

But Ann Aurelia had the answer.

"She's getting married," she announced importantly. "When I went to Eastside two teachers left to get married."

The eyes of the fifth-grade pupils were full of excitement.

"Who's she marrying?" asked Linda. "I've never seen anybody hanging around her. Anybody she would marry. She goes home alone too."

"Maybe it's Mr. Denning," said Dorothy. "He was helping her cross the street when it was slippery this morning."

Linda denied this. "Mr. Denning's got a wife. Mama said she came to P.T.A. with him last meeting."

"Mr. Thornton hasn't," said Ann Aurelia. "Maybe it's him."

"Couldn't be," Dorothy decided wisely. "If she married him, she'd stay on here, and she said she's going away. It must be somebody in the Navy like Hughie. S-sh! Here she comes!"

"Sharing secrets?" asked Miss Bennett lightly.

Donna wriggled uneasily. "We're just talking about the Christmas play. I hope I get a part. I couldn't be in it last year because I had mumps."

"I'm sure you will get a part, and that it will be a splendid play," said Miss Bennett. "You are so good at acting." She looked around the basement. "Has anyone seen Mr. Slocum? I thought our room was a bit chilly this morning."

As if in answer, there was a great thumping and rumbling in the big pipes that ran around the walls.

"He must be down in the furnace room," said Mickey. "I'll go get him."

"Let's play 'prisoner's base,' " suggested Dorothy. "Will you play with us until Mr. Slocum comes, Miss Bennett?"

"I do need a little exercise," said the teacher. "I've been doing too much studying myself lately."

No more mention was made of Miss Bennett's leaving until Dorothy and Ann Aurelia were on their way home.

Dorothy scooped up a handful of snow and began molding it into a ball. "Miss Bennett's been so good to us," she said. "We ought to do something for her. Shirley had a kitchen shower for her best friend before she got married. You should have seen the loot! Five toasters, two electric mixers, and even a fancy apple-peeler."

"Maybe we could give a shower for Miss Bennett."

"We better not do that. Miss Wyckoff always made us take any gifts back. Said it wasn't ethical for a teacher to accept gifts from pupils. But I think it would be ethical to have a surprise party for Miss Bennett before she goes."

"What's ethical?"

"It means doing what you ought to."

"I'll write a poem to read at it. Somebody ought to do that. I wrote a poem once on Mum's birthday and she framed it."

"Maybe Miss Bennett will frame yours. You write such good compositions. But I wish it was some other teacher getting married."

"Like Miss Wyckoff or one of the men. Why does it have to be our Miss Bennett?"

Mrs. Hicken was not too surprised when she heard about the approaching marriage.

"I'm certainly glad for her," she said. "Some of us at P.T.A. have been wondering why such a good-looker as Miss Bennett never got her chance at a man. But we knew it was bound to happen sometime."

Ann Aurelia began to pick at a hangnail on her thumb.

"You won't ever get married again and leave me, will you, Mrs. Hicken?" she anxiously asked.

Mrs. Hicken let out a scornful snort. "Fat chance! Don't ever let that bother your head, Ann Aurelia. Not that I wish to say anything against Mr. Hicken's memory. He was a good provider, and he always stayed home evenings. But he was a fussy man. Always complaining about dust under the beds, and why didn't I defrost the refrigerator before the ice trays got so jammed. I hope Miss Bennett isn't getting a man like that. You don't know who it is, do you?"

"Dorothy and I think it's somebody in the Navy."

"Too bad Mr. Hicken wasn't in the Navy, then he wouldn't have been home so much."

Ann Aurelia and Dorothy gathered the other fifth graders together on the playground. The snow hadn't lasted over the weekend, and it was a clear day.

The girls did most of the planning. The party must be a surprise for Miss Bennett. A big surprise!

"Why do we have to wait till she's about to go?" asked Ann Aurelia. "Why can't we give her the party soon?"

"If we wait too long, somebody's bound to give it away," agreed Dorothy. "Let's have it next Friday after school."

Looking out of a front window in the teachers' room that Friday morning, Miss Bennett noticed that some of the children in her class were awkwardly trying to hide packages.

"Another surprise party," she said to Mr. Denning. "I wonder which one is having a birthday today. The last time it was Donna, but I don't think she was very surprised. Oh, dear, I must look through my desk and see if I can find a suitable present. The children are precious, aren't they? I shall surely miss them."

She left the window and went to her classroom. She pretended not to notice the excited tension that filled the room. When notes were passed, she did not seem to see them. She did not appear to hear all the whispering.

"She doesn't suspect a thing," Dorothy whispered to Ann Aurelia. "You got your poem ready? You didn't lose it, did you?"

"No, it's right on top of the cookies in my desk."

When the last bell rang, the children jumped to their feet, but they did not make a move to leave.

"Surprise, surprise!" called out some of them. Others giggled.

Dorothy stepped from her desk. "We're going to have a little party, Miss Bennett," she announced. "There'll be ice cream and cookies. We've got the cookies in our desks, and the ice cream's down in the cafeteria refrig. But first Ann Aurelia has a poem to read."

Ann Aurelia quickly pulled the sheet of paper from her desk. Surrounded by beaming faces, she read:

PEOPLE YOU LIKE BEST SEEM TO GO AWAY.
WE WISH MISS BENNETT WAS HERE TO STAY.
BUT SHE WILL BE A PRETTY BRIDE,
AND HER HUSBAND WILL BE FULL OF PRIDE.

The children looked at Miss Bennett expectantly. They were delighted to see that she looked even more surprised than they had expected.

Ann Aurelia continued with her poem:

EVEN THOUGH SHE'S MARRIED AND FAR AWAY,
WE'LL TRY TO HAVE GOOD HABITS EVERY DAY.
EVERY FIFTH-GRADE GIRL AND BOY,
WISHES HER AND HER GROOM JOY.

"Congratulations, Miss Bennett. Congratulations!" cried the children.

Miss Bennett looked downright stunned. Her face reddened. She sank into her chair. She rubbed her hand across her forehead. Then she burst into pealing laughter.

"It's the biggest surprise I've ever had," she confessed. "But you've made a mistake. I'm not leaving Jefferson to get married. I'm going back to the university to get another degree. I've been fortunate enough to get a grant that begins this spring."

Ann Aurelia gasped. The poem slipped from her fingers and fell to the floor. She dropped into her seat.

The fifth-grade pupils looked embarrassed and ashamed.

"It was Ann Aurelia said you were getting married," accused Chuck.

"She's the one who started it," cried Donna.

All the fifth-grade pupils, with the exception of Dorothy, pointed accusing fingers at Ann Aurelia.

"It was Ann Aurelia! It was Ann Aurelia!"

They all turned to the door as they heard the knob turn. It burst open to reveal Mrs. Grant bearing a wedding cake. It looked almost as high as a snowbank. On its top layer perched a tiny doll bride and a groom dressed in a sailor suit.

"Here comes the bride," sang Dorothy's mother in her best choir-soprano.

Mrs. Hicken's radiant face appeared from behind the cake.

"Congratulations, Miss Bennett!" she cried.

All of the fifth-grade pupils looked shocked.

Ann Aurelia put her head on her desk and began to weep.

Miss Bennett went to meet the women.

"There has been a little mistake," she said. "I'm not getting married at all. I'm going back to the university to study."

For a moment, Dorothy feared that her mother was going to drop the wedding cake. Mrs. Hicken recovered her wits first. She snatched the bridal pair from the cake and stuffed them into her pocket, even though they were sticky with frosting.

"Please don't be embarrassed," Miss Bennett pleaded. "This is really the biggest surprise I've ever had—and one of the nicest. It would never have happened if Ann Aurelia hadn't supposed that I was getting married. We wouldn't be having this lovely party with this gorgeous wedding cake. I'll wager that you baked it yourself, Mrs. Grant. And I wouldn't have known how much you children like me if it hadn't been for Ann Aurelia's poem."

"Let's start eating," cried Mickey impatiently.

Everyone tried to make the best of things. Mrs. Grant began cutting the cake with the silver knife she had brought. Her fingers trembled as though she were the mother of the bride.

Cookies appeared as if by magic. Chuck and Mickey went to get the ice cream.

It was a party that all the pupils in fifth grade—and Miss Bennett, Mrs. Hicken, and Mrs. Grant—would never forget.

IX

The Unexpected Visitor

Ann Aurelia was sprawled in the big, soft living-room chair doing her homework when the telephone rang.

She went to it and picked up the receiver.

"This is the electric company," said a muffled voice at the other end. "Is your refrigerator running?"

"I'll go see," she answered. She hadn't heard anything about the refrigerator breaking down, but perhaps it had and this was the repair man.

She went to the kitchen and heard the same familiar rattle in Mrs. Hicken's old refrigerator, so she returned to the phone.

"It's still running," she stated.

There were giggles at the other end, and a voice she recognized said, "Then you better run fast and catch it." The receiver on the other end clicked.

Ann Aurelia was annoyed because she had been fooled

by such an old trick. She returned to her homework, but she had hardly settled herself in the chair when the phone jangled again. She returned angrily to the instrument, but the only answer to her "hello" was a burst of giggles.

"I know that's you, Linda Spencer," snapped Ann Aurelia, "and I wish you'd stop bothering me when I'm trying to get my arithmetic done."

She left the receiver off the hook to discourage the prankster.

After the assigned problems had been solved neatly, Ann Aurelia put her books and papers away in her room. With a sigh of relief she returned to the living room and switched on the TV set for that afternoon's western movie.

Just as the sheriff and the bandit faced each other on a dusty road, the doorbell rang.

Ann Aurelia rose in exasperation. Why did people always have to ring the doorbell in the most exciting part of a program? And when Mrs. Hicken was down in the basement going through old newspapers?

She turned the volume higher, then went to the door. When she swung it open, she was surprised to see Miss Watson from the agency. She wasn't due until the next week.

"May I step inside, dear?" asked Miss Watson. "I've

been trying to call you on the phone, but I kept getting the busy signal."

"Of course, Miss Watson. Will you take off your coat while I put the receiver back on the hook. I guess I left it off."

"I'll keep my coat this time, Ann Aurelia," answered Miss Watson. "We won't be here long."

There must be somebody waiting in the car. That was a good thing. Miss Watson would surely leave soon.

Miss Watson put her hands to her ears. "Will you please turn that off? I want to talk to you."

"I was just going to," said Ann Aurelia. She obediently went to the TV set. She stood a moment watching the bandit and the sheriff shooting at each other from behind rocks. Then she pushed the button.

"Is Mrs. Hicken here?" asked Miss Watson.

"She's looking through old papers for a recipe she forgot to tear out."

"Coming," said Mrs. Hicken's voice from the top of the basement steps. She walked into the room, carrying a newspaper in her hand. "Miss Watson!" she exclaimed. "What a nice surprise!"

She quickly laid the paper across the undusted surface of the end table.

"I've come to get Ann Aurelia," said Miss Watson.

"She has a visitor at the Home."

"Oh, of course! Get your coat, dearie. The house may look a little upset, Miss Watson, because cleaning day isn't until tomorrow."

"Shall I change into a dress?" asked Ann Aurelia, looking down at her slacks.

She was boiling with curiosity, but she didn't want the women to notice.

"There isn't time since I couldn't get you by phone," said Miss Watson. "But you might wash your hands and run a comb through your hair."

"Yes, ma'am."

After performing these duties, Ann Aurelia followed Miss Watson to the car. She was strangled by fear and doubt. Who was the visitor? Was it a new foster mother? Were they going to take her away from Mrs. Hicken? Panicky thoughts fluttered through her head like frightened birds caught in a net.

When they were in the car, Miss Watson said, "Your mother has come back, Ann Aurelia. I know you will be happy to see her again."

Ann Aurelia was too stunned to think clearly. She tried to understand the full meaning of what Miss Watson had said. Had Mum come for just a visit, or were she and Mr. Lacey moving back here? If only she had known sooner, she would have been prepared to meet whatever was waiting for her. If it hadn't been for that Linda Spencer's telephone tricks! She began twisting the button on her coat because she couldn't think of anything to say to Miss Watson.

Miss Watson was silent too, as she steered the car toward the Home. Usually she was busy asking such questions as "What did you have for breakfast, dear?" and "How do you like Jefferson School? Are you still making good marks?"

The automobile stopped in front of a great square building that dwarfed those around it. It looked as forbidding to Ann Aurelia as it had that first time, over a year ago. She remembered that unhappy day when Mum and Mr. Lacey had brought her here, saying they would come back for her after their honeymoon.

She remembered the time when she had been about Louise's age and had been lost in a big department store. She had cried bitterly because she had never expected to see Mum again. The people who gathered around her had tried to be kind, but she didn't want strangers—she wanted her own mother. That was the way she felt when she watched Mum and Mr. Lacey drive away.

Miss Watson remained silent until they were inside the heavy oak door. Then she said, "Take off your coat, Ann

Aurelia, and then come to the south parlor. I'll be waiting for you there."

Dutifully Ann Aurelia hung her woolen coat on a peg over the antique umbrella stand that someone had donated to the Home long ago. She went to the door of the south parlor. She hesitated a moment; then firmly turned the knob and walked inside.

A strange-looking woman was sitting on the lumpy sofa. Her face was tense and pale under smooth brown hair.

She returned Ann Aurelia's look with a blank stare. Her eyes rested on the short hair of the child who appeared to be a gangling little boy.

"Hello, Mum," said Ann Aurelia in a low voice.

The woman jumped to her feet. "Ann Aurelia! I didn't know you." She spoke in a soft, wondering voice. "You look so different."

"You look different too," said Ann Aurelia.

Her mother held out her arms. "Can't you give me a big hug and kiss?"

Ann Aurelia walked slowly to her. But she turned her face away as her mother hugged her, and her own arms hung limply at her side.

Mum backed to the sofa and pulled Ann Aurelia down beside her.

"Aren't you glad to see me?" she asked anxiously.

"Sure." Ann Aurelia rubbed her right eye as if there were something in it.

"You got the green pin I sent you for Christmas, didn't you?"

Ann Aurelia rubbed her eye harder. "I gave it to Mrs. Hicken for her birthday because she didn't have anybody else to give her presents."

Her mother's face flushed, but she continued in a bright manner, "Why didn't you answer any of my letters?"

"I had school work to do."

"You were always a good student."

Ann Aurelia's eyes brightened. "I got 'A' in everything." Then her voice changed. "Mrs. Hicken signs my report cards. She's proud of my 'A's."

"I'll be signing them now and I'll be proud too." Mum paused as if trying to find the right words. "Mr. Lacey and I aren't together anymore. I missed you, and when I saw he hadn't meant for you to come back it didn't work out. It will be just you and me again."

Ann Aurelia beamed and she moved closer to her mother. Then her eyes clouded.

"Maybe you'll marry somebody else and go away again."

Mum's voice was unsteady when she said, "I'll never leave you again. I promise."

Ann Aurelia still looked worried. "But Mrs. Hicken—" she said, "she won't want me to leave her."

Mum bit her lip. "It shouldn't make any difference to her."

"Yes, it will," declared Ann Aurelia, moving away from her mother. "I know it will. She bakes cakes for me specially and helps me with my homework—and she takes me to movies."

Mum said lightly, "She'd do the same for any other child. She's only been boarding you for pay, you know."

Ann Aurelia's face contorted and she jumped up. "She even joined the P.T.A. for me. She wanted me and you didn't. I belong to Mrs. Hicken now."

She turned and ran out of the room.

"Ann—dear—please—" her mother called.

In the hall, Miss Watson stepped between them.

"Give her time, Mrs. Lacey," she said. "This has been quite a shock for her. I'll drive her back to Mrs. Hicken now."

As she followed Miss Watson to the door, Ann Aurelia stuck her fingers tightly into her ears. She didn't want to hear her mother's sobs.

When the car turned the corner, shutting off sight of the Home, Miss Watson said, "We don't expect you to make up your mind in a hurry, Ann Aurelia. What you decide will have a great influence on whether the court returns you to your mother or keeps you under our jurisdiction."

Ann Aurelia bowed her head. "I've already decided. I want to stay with Mrs. Hicken."

"You have decided too fast," admonished Miss Watson. "You haven't had time to consider everything. You must think about it more. Each side must be weighed. Mrs. Hicken is a fine woman but Mrs. Lacey is your mother."

"She left me."

"She told me that she had made a terrible mistake," said Miss Watson. "She really believed Mr. Lacey loved you or she wouldn't have married him. Everyone is human, Ann Aurelia. Even mothers."

Ann Aurelia began to take a great interest in a loose thread on her coat.

Miss Watson went on. "You must consider the other side too, of course. Mrs. Hicken is fond of you. She has treated you like her own child, and you are doing well in her care. Better than you did with the Swanns or Mr. and Mrs. Jolly."

"I want to stay with her," persisted Ann Aurelia as she

twisted the thread.

"You mustn't make a quick decision before thinking over all aspects of this. The court will give you time. Just consider that, on one hand, Mrs. Lacey is your natural mother who really loves you deeply. Also consider that the relationship between you and Mrs. Hicken has been ideal. You might talk with her about it."

Ann Aurelia found Mrs. Hicken's advice as confusing as that of Miss Watson.

"She *is* your mother, dearie," she agreed with Miss Watson. "But that's my hard luck. I've had to look after foster children to make both ends meet ever since Mr. Hicken died. But I've got no complaint coming, mind you. And, of all the children I've ever boarded, I've liked you best. I'll say it now, Ann Aurelia, then take my nose out of it. I've loved you just like you were my own—or I wouldn't have joined the P.T.A."

"And you're the best mother I've *ever* had," declared Ann Aurelia staunchly. But she felt as if she were in a tug-of-war game with one player pulling her this way and the other that way. There was only one person whose advice she could trust.

"May I go to see Dorothy for a little while?" she asked. "I want her to look over my arithmetic problems to see if I got them right."

"Sure, dearie," said Mrs. Hicken, "but don't stay over there for dinner again. They'll be getting tired of you. And I'll make hot biscuits tonight. They're a lot of trouble, but you're so crazy about them. I'll go to the supermarket and get some of that black-cherry ice cream too."

Mrs. Hicken put a plump arm around Ann Aurelia and gave her a squeeze. "Now don't you worry about anything," she said soothingly. "You'll have even worse problems when you grow up."

Dorothy was astonished to hear about the return of Ann Aurelia's mother. Her eyes widened and her mouth dropped open.

"It's like that movie we saw last week where the little boy found out that the policeman at the school crossing was his real, honest father."

"Movies are silly," said Ann Aurelia. "I'm not going back to her. And I don't think they'll make me."

"Then you've got no worry. You can keep on staying with Mrs. Hicken—if that's what you want."

Ann Aurelia began to draw a face on her thumbnail with her pencil. "Mum told Miss Watson she'd made a big mistake."

"We've made plenty of mistakes ourselves, A. A. Remember how we fooled around with the safety flags and got put off the Patrol? And that time we played house in the supermarket? We could have gone to jail maybe."

"But she made a whopping mistake. And now she expects me to forgive her."

"We made a whopper when we had that surprise party for Miss Bennett. I thought Mama never would forgive *me*."

"But the worst was when Mum said Mrs. Hicken just keeps me because she gets paid for it. And Mrs. Hicken told me herself that she loves me."

Dorothy deliberated for a few moments. "That was just because she doesn't know Mrs. Hicken like we do. Some of the kids' parents think Miss Bennett just teaches us because she gets paid. But we know she really likes us a lot too. Mrs. Hicken and Miss Bennett can get other kids to like, but you're your mother's only real, honest child."

Ann Aurelia began erasing the face on her thumbnail.

"If I go back to Mum, I'll probably have to leave Jefferson. And I won't have you around anymore."

"You have to take things as they come, A. A. If we moved away, I'd have to leave you. I'd hate to, but I'd want to be with my own mother and family. Hughie went off and joined the Navy, but he comes home every chance he gets."

Ann Aurelia ran the pencil point back and forth across her thumbnail to blacken it. "Miss Watson talked as if I should go back to Mum. Then she talked as if I should stay with Mrs. Hicken. Grownups get you all mixed up. They're always full of reasons for everything."

"I haven't got any reasons, A. A.," said Dorothy. "I just think you should go back because she's your real, honest mother."

Ann Aurelia's eyes had a faraway look in them. "You know, Dorothy, Mum looked lonesome and scared in the parlor—like some of the little kids when they first get brought to the Home."

"You looked pretty lonesome that first day you bumped into me in the park."

"I felt lonesome too. That must be the way Mum feels now. I really want to go back to her, but I hate to hurt Mrs. Hicken's feelings."

X

The Apartment

I want to go straight home to see how Mum has fixed up our new apartment," said Ann Aurelia to Dorothy as they set their Patrol flags against the wall. "You'll come with me, won't you?"

"For just a minute," answered Dorothy. "Mama says I must hurry home. I have to watch Louise while she goes to that committee meeting. It's at Mrs. Hicken's now that she's secretary of the P.T.A."

"Wasn't it nice of Mrs. Hicken to find us an apartment so close to school? Another P.T.A. lady told her about it. Thought we'd never get to move out of that old hotel."

"I guess Mrs. Hicken didn't want you going too far away where she'd never see you again," reasoned Dorothy. "And your mum wanted you to keep on at Jefferson."

They bounded down the school steps, two at a time.

"Mrs. Hicken's going to get another girl from the Home. Wonder what she'll be like? We can play with her when she comes so she won't be as lonesome as I was at first," said Ann Aurelia.

They soon reached a great barn-like house with brown clapboards and faded yellow trim. Ann Aurelia paused on the sidewalk and clasped her hands.

"Isn't it the grandest?" she asked. "Doesn't it look just like a mansion?"

Dorothy stared at the house dubiously. "I know how you feel, A. A.," she conceded. "Our house is little and there's hardly any yard, but I think it's the best one in town because Daddy bought it for us. And now that you'll be living here with your mum, you won't care if some of the clapboards are off and the paint around the windows is peeling."

"But come and see the big back yard," urged Ann Aurelia. "Mrs. Murphy says I can play in it all I want. And we've got our own door—just like the whole house belonged to us."

Dorothy followed her across the broken flagstone walk. "And there's a cat." She pointed at a gray tabby sunning herself near the bottom of a crooked downspout. "Does she belong to you?"

"She must belong to Mrs. Murphy, but I'm going to give her milk every morning so she'll think she belongs to me. Nobody could have pets at the hotel. And Mrs. Hicken couldn't have any around because they made her sneeze or something."

After a quick pat of the cat's head that brought forth a rewarding purr, Ann Aurelia led Dorothy up a long flight of outside stairs to the second-floor apartment. The cat followed them and then contentedly settled herself on the landing.

Ann Aurelia's mother came to greet them. She was hastily zipping her housedress.

"I just got back from the beauty parlor," she explained. "Hello, Dorothy. Come in and see our new apartment now that the furniture has come from the storage company."

Dorothy walked around on tiptoe as if she were in a museum. Ann Aurelia explained everything as if she were the guide.

"And there's our sofa that opens into a bed. Maybe you can spend the night with me sometime. And my old desk! I can do my lessons here." She squeezed into the seat with some effort. "I must have grown taller."

Dorothy admired everything, but the bedroom interested her most. "That dressing table is just like Shirley's. And you even have pink curtains."

"I only had time to hang one pair before I went to the beauty parlor," explained Mum. She ran her long fingernails through her brown hair. "Had a shampoo and golden rinse. The girl wanted to bleach it again, but I think I'll leave it the way it is."

"I like it now," said Ann Aurelia. "Like it was when I was real little."

Dorothy caught sight of the alarm clock on the dressing table. "I've got to run," she declared. "See you at school tomorrow, A. A. And don't be late playing with that cat."

After Dorothy's departure, Ann Aurelia explored further among the household items which she hadn't seen for so long.

"Here's that picture you took of me when I was a baby in my playpen!" she exclaimed. She studied the framed enlargement critically. "I wasn't much to look at, was I? Skinny and baldheaded."

"I thought you were beautiful," said Mum with a laugh. "I remember how insulted I was when a neighbor said you were so ugly that you were cute."

"Tell me more about when I was a baby, Mum," begged Ann Aurelia. "Mrs. Hicken didn't know anything about then. She often talked to me about when she was a baby herself. She got her head caught between the crib bars and the firemen had to come and get her loose. And one time she won third prize in a baby contest because she was so plump and healthy-looking. But she didn't know anything about me when I was little."

Mum wrinkled her forehead as she tried to remember something new. "You were three years old before you even began to talk, and it worried me. But once you started, I thought you'd never stop."

"Remember the time I got lost from you in the store? I wouldn't talk to any of those strange ladies who tried to help me, and I almost bawled my head off. You don't know how awful I felt."

Mum's face sobered.

"Yes, I do, Ann Aurelia," she confessed. "I've been lost, too, but now we've found each other again. We'll do lots of fun things to make up for the time we lost. How would you like to take Dorothy with us to River Park next Saturday? We can go on the bus and make a day of it."

Ann Aurelia clapped her hands. "And take a picnic lunch. And we'll show you where Miss Wyckoff almost drowned herself."

It was May. A feverish restlessness had come over the pupils of Jefferson School. They were beginning to talk about vacation and playground programs and summer trips.

"I wish Miss Reese would hurry up and let us start

practicing for the June pageant," said Ann Aurelia.

"We've asked her about it a dozen times," said Dorothy, "but she keeps saying it's too early yet."

"She's really the greatest though, isn't she?"

"And pretty as Miss Bennett. Maybe a little stricter, but she thinks up such exciting things to do."

"And the pageant sounds super. Mum can hardly wait to see me in it."

The girls skipped along the sidewalk. Above them the chestnut trees were trimmed with popcorn blossoms, and all the front yards on West Street were emerald-green squares framed in bright flower borders.

"Aren't you glad that you went back with your mum after all?" asked Dorothy.

"Sure am. You know, Dorothy, I found out she really needs me. I run errands for her and make up the beds every day and tell her jokes when she looks sad. I thought it was only children who needed their mothers. And I was mad all along and trying to show I could do without her."

Dorothy nodded understandingly. "Mama and I both need each other. And I bet right now Louise needs you and me."

"She's probably sitting on the porch waiting for us," guessed Ann Aurelia.

"Ever since we told her we'd take her to play with

Kathy again, she's been pestering me."

"Once you promise little kids something, they bother you to death about it."

As Ann Aurelia had predicted, Louise was sitting on the front steps of the Grant house. In her arms was a rag doll that was worn and torn by love and play.

At sight of the two girls, the child jumped up and went running to meet them. "You said you'd take me to see Kathy. Pam and I are ready."

"You've been ready for the last three days," grumbled Dorothy. "Come on! We'll take you there to shut you up." She took Louise by her free hand. "Remember to be polite to Kathy, and let her play with Pam too."

They went down the street, Louise taking little hops and skips to keep up with her sister. Because the sidewalk was narrow, Ann Aurelia walked in the gutter.

When they came to Mrs. Hicken's house, they turned into the walk. Ann Aurelia rang the bell.

"I feel funny doing this," she said. "I used to walk right in the back door."

Mrs. Hicken answered the bell with a wary look, as if she expected to be talked into buying something she didn't want.

"Oh, it's you two," she greeted them. "And little Louise. Now won't Kathy be happy! She's been after me to take her to see Louise. Come right in."

A little girl of Louise's age wriggled out of the big chair and joined them. She had a pointed elfin face and blunt sausage curls. She looked at Louise shyly.

"Hi, Kathy!" said Louise. She held out the battered doll. "You can hold Pam. I'll be the father."

"Now aren't they a pair!" exclaimed Mrs. Hicken. "Last time neither one wanted to be the father. Come here, dearie," she coaxed Kathy. "Let me fix that back curl. It's coming loose." She pulled the child to her and twisted the offending curl around her finger. "It's a nuisance to make them every morning, but they keep her face from looking so peaked. Your hair's grown out a lot, Ann Aurelia."

Ann Aurelia fluffed her thick waves with her fingers. "It came out curly too. It never was before it was cut."

"You're as pretty as Miss Reese," Dorothy complimented her, "and you look just like a girl. No wonder Mickey Ryan aimed his new spaceship at you this morning."

Kathy tugged at Mrs. Hicken's skirt. "Can we play house with cookies, Mama?" she asked.

Mrs. Hicken's face shone. "She's so little she thinks I'm her mother. Her own is dead, and her father works nights. Yes, dearie, Mama will get the cookies for you right away. I'll give you girls some too; then you'll be free to go and play. I'll mind Louise."

Ann Aurelia and Dorothy munched the sugar cookies as they headed for the playground.

"I can't play long," warned Ann Aurelia. "I promised Mum to get back to the apartment and set the table for dinner and start things cooking. She's at the lawyer's changing her name back to Wilson."

"I like that better. And it won't sound like you're just her foster child. I'll help you so we can talk about the pageant some more."

"Let's surprise Mum with something different," suggested Ann Aurelia.

"Not like that rice we made when she went to the sale. Remember how we had to keep getting extra pans to put it in? *Glap!* I never did see stuff swell up so much."

"I know what. Let's not go to the playground at all. Let's go straight to the apartment and make up a batch of cookies. That would be a nice surprise for Mum. You can have some too."

"That's a super idea, A. A. But let's make them different from these Mrs. Hicken gave us."

"We'll make a real special kind of cookie," added Ann Aurelia excitedly. "Let's put blue coloring in the dough, and maybe sprinkle grapenuts on top. And no telling what else we can scrape up in the pantry."